Secrets

John Callas

Copyright © 2021 by John Callas
ISBN: 978-1-7367127-2-6

Editor:
Karl Monger
www.karlmonger.com

Cover Design:
AdMark Group
http://admarkgroup.com/#/home/

Marlena Brown
marlenabrown.com

AUTHOR'S NOTE

While this story is largely a fiction, the events during World War II and what has been proposed in this novel are true.

Many Nazis fled to the US and found high level and influential position within our own government and began a fifty-year war from within. This strategy included convincing a vast majority of society that drugs are needed for afflictions that have shown to be less intrusive than the prescribe drug's side effects.

Mind control was high on the Nazi list to accomplish. A practice that all governments now do intensive research. Hitler commented in Mein Kampf that the way to control the masses is through physical and mental terror. Mind control is part of that momentum.

Today's news only confirms that the shift in what our country use to stand for has and continues to erode. "Secrets" opens the door to examine some of the things that are in play today that can be directly linked back to World War II and the Nazi party.

DEDICATION

For Mom, Dad,
and
My loving and supportive family
Linda, Stephan, and Nicholas

ACKNOWLEDGMENTS

Additional cover design by Kim Barton
http://www.tymecaptured.com

FOREWORD

"Single acts of tyranny may be ascribed to the accidental opinion of the day, but a series of oppressions begun at a distinguished period, unalterable through every change of ministers, too plainly prove a deliberate, systematic plan of reducing us to slavery."

"The spirit of resistance to government is so valuable on certain occasions that I wish it to be always kept alive."

Thomas Jefferson 1774

"Some of the biggest men in the United States, in the field of commerce and manufacture, are afraid of somebody, are afraid of something. They know there is a power somewhere, so organized, so subtle, so watchful, so interlocked, so pervasive, that they had better not speak above their breath in condemnation of it"

"We have come to be one of the worst ruled, one of the most controlled and dominated governments in the civilized world. No government by free opinion, no longer a government by conviction and the vote of the majority, but a government by the opinion and the duress of small groups of dominant men."

Woodrow Wilson 1919

"All great movements are popular movements. They are the volcanic eruptions of human passions and emotions, stirred into activity by the ruthless Goddess of Distress or by the torch of the spoken word cast into the midst of the people. What good fortune for governments that the people do not think."

"By means of shrewd lies, unremittingly repeated, it is possible to make people believe that heaven is hell and hell heaven. The greater the lie, the more readily it will be believed."

Adolf Hitler 1939

ONE

The snow drifts silently through the dry night air. It is so cold outside that it hurts to breathe, each breath paining the lungs while drawing the nostrils closed for a short time until the body heat warms them up, ready for the next painful breath. The trees testify to the harshness of the dismal winters these woods have endured. Each branch, encased in ice, droops, waiting in desperation for spring to once again usher in warmth and life. If not for a few scattered tracks in the snow, it would be easy to imagine that animal life could not possibly exist in such a harsh land. It is against this dismal setting that the Nazis unleash their assault on Europe.

In a remote post in this frozen land, several guards, half-frozen and near starvation, hear the telltale rumble of an approaching vehicle. The densely packed snow creaks under the pressure of the car's tires as they roll steadily toward the outpost. Icicles cling to the running boards of the car, occasionally falling off. The wiper blades squeak across the moist windshield, gradually breaking up the melting snow and giving way to glimpses of the interior. A convoy of high-ranking Nazi officials dressed in heavy overcoats fill the plush leather seats, smoking in silence in the comfort of their heated vehicle. They pass around a silver flask, with each man taking a sip. The one-hundred-year-old cognac imparts a welcome burning sensation that registers on the face of each man. The plush leather seats add to the comfort and luxury that only the privileged few enjoy.

Despite his soft facial features, Colonel Von Schlieg would rather tear your heart out than say good morning. The details of his appearance--the flowing black hair, full lips, beady eyes, shoulders that look like a piece of wood is holding them straight, and flanged nose--are the last things many an unfortunate soul registers before their lives are forever changed, always for the worse. His reputation for cruelty precedes him, as does his preference for aiming it at Jewish children, often using them like foxes for his personal inhuman hunts. He likes to boast of more than a thousand confirmed kills.

The car's headlights carve a path through the otherwise complete darkness, illuminating the snowflakes as they succumb gracefully to gravity. The snow drifts past the windows, swirling faster and faster and colliding into a rooster tail behind the car before drifting into the void of darkness. Turning the corner, the faint outline of an isolated guard shack in the distance comes into view.

The shivering guards come out of the shed with readied weapons to meet the approaching vehicle. Each man adjusts his coat to keep the snow from sneaking down his neck. Helmet straps are tightly secured beneath chins as the men constantly shuffle their feet in an attempt to prevent frostbite from taking hold. The men exchange looks of anxious anticipation. Knowing that during war, anything can and does happen, they are on guard against the unexpected. Nerves are raw and fingers are frozen. Two men light cigarettes and draw deeply, hoping each puff isn't their last. The car slowly comes into view. The Nazi flags on the bumpers are clearly displayed. As if rehearsed countless times, the men take their positions. The lowered gate meets the headlights, and the car comes to a stop. The guards surround the car according to their strict training procedures. One guard marches over to the driver. They speak in German.

"Papers, please," comes the request. The other guards eye the passengers and then look at each other. Fingertips caress triggers. The rear driver's side window is lowered.

"What is the meaning of this?" bellows Col. Von Schlieg. "We have to be at headquarters in thirty minutes."

"Sorry for the inconvenience, sir, but I have my orders. I need to see your papers," answers the guard closest to him.

Outraged, Col. Von Schlieg steps out of the warm car and into the falling snow. The driver gets out and looks at the other guards. The two other officials remain in the car.

"The papers are inside the glove box," answers the driver.

The guard waves his machine gun at the driver. "Get them."

Col. Von Schlieg's eyes narrow. "No, do not get the papers." He swivels his ice-cold gaze to the guard. "Now, let us pass or you will find yourself on the front lines… or worse."

The guards assume rigid stances. It is a classic standoff. Eyes strain to keep from blinking. Time freezes. Tension mounts. Snow continues falling softly and silently. The driver throws Col. Von Schlieg a questioning look. Col. Von Schlieg becomes impatient and reaches for his side arm. The two men eye each other. Time seems to slow as he unfastens the leather strap restraining his Luger. He eases it out of its holster. The guard nearest Von Schlieg sees the Luger and reacts. Suddenly the stillness of the night is shattered by the sound of machine gun fire. The driver and Col. Von Schlieg fall hard to the ground, dead. Before the other two passengers can react, a machine gun is stuck inside the car. The rapid strobe of muzzle flashes silhouettes the spasms of the lead-filled bodies as screams echo through the frozen woods. Silence returns. The first guard to react turns to his compatriot and speaks in English.

"Sam, get the uniforms."

"Right."

He goes behind the guard shed and pulls out a few duffel bags. Inside are clean, pressed Nazi uniforms, identical to the ones of the now dead officials. Checking the map and going over last-minute details, the five men get in the car and drive into the night.

An hour later the car approaches Berlin, the stronghold of the Nazi Reich. Massive stone buildings jut into the sky, intimidating in their dark monotony. The air is so thick with the scents of death and distrust that citizens and soldiers alike become unwitting victims of war. The soul of the country has been sucked dry, its own people turning one another in for expressing any opinion not sanctioned by the Reich. Parents no longer trust their children. Children have learned to distrust their parents and report dissident thinking. They have been taught that the Reich and the Fatherland are the only things that matter. They must be willing to die for their country. Hitler has assumed the role of father to all German children. He is the only parent they will know and love. He is a God to them, a God who fell from the graces of heaven to rule in hell. A hell on earth that the countries of the world have come to know as Nazi Germany.

Amid the buildings draped with immense swastika banners, guards patrolling with dogs, and searchlights sweeping the sky and grounds, the car pulls to a stop in front of Nazi headquarters. The assassins, now dressed in high-ranking Nazi uniforms, get out of the car. The guards posted at the entrance examine their papers. Satisfied, they escort the imposters into the building.

A string of bare light bulbs illuminates the dark, ice-laced walls of stone from overhead. Armed soldiers escort the assassins down the hall. The cold air captures the warm breath of each man as the echo of boot heels striking the cold concrete floor drowns out the silence. The line of breath dissolves as each man moves forward with purpose, heading for an unknown destination.

In precise military fashion, the escorts stop in front of a huge three-foot-thick steel door. After a series of knocks the door slowly opens. Papers are once again proffered, reviewed, approved, and handed back before they enter. The room is impressive in its Germanic organization. Everything is perfectly ordered and appropriately placed, and the equipment is state of the art.

SLAM! The steel door shuts and locks. Two armed guards stand inside the soundproof room with watchful eyes. Everyone in the room raises their arms in salute.

"Heil Hitler."

"Colonel Von Schlieg, it is an honor to finally meet you. My name is Eric Gestling. I trust you had a comfortable trip?"

The assassin looks around the room and finally answers. "Yes. And now I would like to get to work."

"Of course."

Eric Gestling turns toward the conference table presenting the perfectly stacked and ordered files awaiting the arrival of the real Col. Von Schlieg.

"Here are the papers for your team to go through. I need not remind you of their sensitive nature."

The assassin turns to face Gestling, who knows of the colonel's fierce reputation.

"And I need not remind you, Herr Gestling, of who I am and how easy it is to become a casualty of war?"

"No, sir."

"Good. Then you and the guards can leave us in private."

"But sir, my orders..."

Before the man can finish his sentence, the imposter draws his sidearm and shoots one of the guards in the forehead. Blood drips down the wall behind the guard as he sinks to the floor. One of the other assassins draws on the other guard.

"Next time I have to repeat myself it will be you."

Gestling and the remaining guard leave the room without another word. Once the door is shut, the assassins speak in English. The leader, Gus, turns to his men.

"Sam, start looking for the files we are to replace."

"On it."

"Neil, go through the last communications and see what you can find out."

"You want the tapes or just notes?"

"Just notes. We don't want them to suspect that anything has been changed."

Each man has been charged with a specific mission, and taken together the missions are designed to send the Nazis in the wrong direction for the D-Day invasion. And when the deception finally comes to light, blame will fall on the Nazi high command and heads will quite literally roll. The truth of the swap will forever remain a secret, and so far the mission has been executed to perfection. Every minute brings each man closer to the time when he will be back in America and in his family's arms. Silently they work, their minds focused on their assignments and their hearts filled with thoughts of home.

Far away, unanticipated events are beginning to unfold, starting with the guard shack. The isolated shack is the turnkey to the operation. Assassinating the colonel was their passport to a successful operation. Killing the guards was supposed to be the easy part. All had gone according to plan... except for one fatal oversight.

The snow is falling heavier on and around the guard shack as the bloody trails left by the dragged bodies continue to disappear. Inside are the bullet-riddled corpses of the guards. Each body has stiffened into a macabre position that tells the gruesome tale of its last breath of life. Twisted and broken, some of the soldiers' hands clawed the walls in fear and desperation. One faceless body slumping over the desk looks almost peaceful. The body lying next to the doorway was the first victim of the assassins as they entered the shed. Pummeled by a barrage of machine gun fire, the body flew across the room, striking the solid concrete wall. Family pictures that once hung on the walls now lie bloodstained and broken on the floor. The quietude of death is so deafening that each snowflake sounds like a drop of water hitting a hot skillet. With the body heat of each soldier dissipating, the frigid temperature becomes the embalming fluid that will preserve them until spring brings thawing...and decay.

On the ring finger of the youngest soldier is a shiny new wedding band. Married only one week before going to war, he still recalls the taste of the wedding cake and the last passionate night spent with his new bride before coming to this frozen wasteland. What he assumes will be his last thought is the music playing as her long black hair falls across his chest. He still can feel her soft skin against the palm of his hand as it moves slowly down her lower back in the candlelit room. Looking deeply into her eyes he can almost feel the touch of her full lips against his, her mouth hungrily engulfing his lower lip, their tongues swirling around each other in wet passion. Her nipples are hard and yearning. Her movement against his masculine expression sends them both into a blissful orgasm that was supposed to carry him safely through the war and back to her loving arms. It is an image of hope and a dream of things to come as they fall into an exhausted sleep, hands clasped, never wanting to let go.

The first movement of his hand is involuntary, a result of the cooling of the body. Then his legs begin to move. His internal organs, having escaped the delivery of death, strive to reestablish life. His chest moves up and down with each revitalizing breath. His eyes flicker open. Blood sprays out of his mouth as he coughs for air and life. Half-frozen and on the verge of death, he grapples for the phone. The quivering bloodstained hand begins a determined attempt to dial headquarters. The same headquarters where Gus and his men carry out their mission.

Gus surveys the enormous, well-organized room, impressed by the sense of military precision that only another soldier could appreciate in wartime. The room's hand-carved fixtures have been executed per the rigorous standards of the finest German craftsmanship. Momentarily dazed by the beauty of the work, Gus runs his hand over the carvings. The inlaid beveled mirror imparts a simple and expansive elegance to the room. Admiring the frame, Gus notices a piece of wood that seems slightly crooked. As he gently pushes the piece back into place, the wall slides open. The soft scraping sound that ensues causes everyone in the room to freeze in place. Instinctively, the men grab their weapons, ready for a fight. The mirrored wall fully opens to reveal a ten-foot by ten-foot room. In the center of the room is a desk, and on top of the desk is a lamp illuminating the desk's only contents, a single file folder stuffed with papers. Gus peeks cautiously into the room.

Turning to his men, he says, "Relax, it's clear."

The men return to their mission as Gus enters the room. He sits behind the desk and looks at the six-inch-thick file. Gus opens the file and proceeds to read, his eyes growing wide in disbelief. The report he is reading verges on science-fiction, but as he learned a long time ago, documents speak for themselves. Goosebumps sprout on his arms the more he reads. He turns page after page, his fascination turning to fear, but still he cannot stop reading. The deeper he goes the more outrageous it becomes. Completely absorbed in the file, he doesn't notice that Neil has entered the room.

"We have to leave in ten minutes to stay on schedule."

As Gus looks up from the file, Neil sees the horror in his eyes. He has never seen Gus shaken by anything.

"Whatever it is you found, read fast 'cause we're out of here in ten."

Neil leaves the room as Gus takes out a miniature camera. He begins photographing the file while the men wrap up their mission. Gus's mind continues to race. What if everything he just read is true? What if they can actually accomplish what they propose in these documents? Who could possibly stop such a plan? How did it ever get to this point? He pauses to reload the camera. Only five more pages to go.

Neil looks at his watch. They are out of time. He goes to retrieve Gus. As he reaches the room, Gus comes out and closes the mirrored wall.

"Is everyone ready, Neil?"

"Yes, sir."

"Good. Let's get the hell out of here and go home."

"Sounds good to me."

On the main floor of the compound a phone rings. The orderly answers the call as Gus and his men pass by on the way to their car, which will take them back home and to safety. Looking up, the orderly drops the phone and runs to an alarm. Its piercing sound shrieks throughout the compound.

The orderly yells, "HALT."

Gus and the squad immediately realize their cover has been blown. Sam turns and silences the orderly with a single bullet through the head.

Outside Paul stands next to the car, nervously pacing as the alarm continues screeching. He thinks to himself, Should I wait, or leave and report back to base? Are the others dead, and will I be next if I wait any longer? It seems his only hope of survival is to jump in the car and drive as fast as he can to safety. The two guards standing at the entrance look at each other, confused by Paul's erratic behavior. Their attention shifts to the building as they are distracted by the blaring sirens. For a split second they turn their backs to him, and Paul reaches into the car and retrieves a machine gun. As the guards turn back to Paul, he cuts them down, opening the escape route for his unit, which just comes into view.

"Sam, buy us some time!" shouts Gus.

"Got it."

Sam stops and pulls out a few grenades from under his jacket. As he does so, a soldier sees him and opens fire. Sam falls to the ground but manages to get the grenades out. The soldier walks up to him and is about to deliver the coup de grace when he sees the grenades Sam is holding. Sam smiles at the soldier, who turns to run. Five grenades roll to the feet of the now fleeing soldier. The explosion sends debris flying in every direction, killing the soldier and sealing the hallway.

The remaining men run outside and see Paul waiting by the car. Another German soldier comes around the building and opens fire. Paul falls over the hood of the car. The men turn and simultaneously shoot the soldier. Gus runs to Paul, but it is too late. Paul takes hold of Gus's hand and dies. Gus pulls off Paul's dog tags and jumps into the car. Gunfire erupts all around them. They are pinned.

"Get in the car," yells Gus.

One by one they are picked off until everyone is dead except for Neil and Gus. They speed out of the compound, bullets flying all around them. A Nazi vehicle with an armed machine gun is in hot pursuit. Two pairs of headlight beams illuminate the dark road. Gus turns to Neil. "No matter what happens, headquarters has to get this information."

"What did you find, Gus?" Neil is breathing hard, rocked by the sudden realization he may never see his family again.

Gus keeps his eyes glued to the road while maneuvering icy curves.

"I photographed documents proving that..."

A bullet shatters the windshield into a million razor projectiles looking for a target. Gus looks back to see how close they are getting. It is when he turns back that he notices something is wrong. What is left of Neil's head is leaning on the top of the seat. In his blood-soaked hand is a picture of his wife and their two small children. Gus looks at the road. A sharp turn next to a steep ravine is coming up fast. He grabs his dead partner's dog tags, a machine gun, and a map, and he jumps out of the jeep. He rolls head over heels to the side of the road and finally comes to a stop. He is badly bruised but alive.

The pursuers speed past Gus without noticing him. Gus's jeep flies over the side of the mountain, plummeting to the bottom, where upon impact it explodes in a ball of fire. The Nazis stop, quickly exit their vehicle, look over the edge, and laugh. Satisfied, they turn to leave, and without warning they are peppered with machine gun fire. Gus's eyes are pools of rage as he fires on the soldiers until the surrounding woods echo with only the clicking sound of the firing pins striking against empty chambers. Gus lets go of the trigger and clutches Neil's dog tags in his hand as he looks up at the night sky in search of answers.

TWO

Toward the end of the war, Gus and his wife Pauline are approached by an officer and longtime friend with an offer to engage in post-war intelligence work. The opportunity is as well paid as it is exciting.

"Your offer is very tempting, and Pauline and I will discuss it and let you know our decision. But I don't understand why the department has no interest in pursuing the information that I uncovered in Berlin."

The officer shifts his eyes uncomfortably around the room. "I know how you feel, Gus. I feel the same way. The truth is there is a good deal of posturing in the intelligence game. Many times there are few if any of us who will ever know the truth of why certain things work the way they do. There are players and forces out there that control our every move. I don't know how it came to be this way or who conceived it first. Hell, it could have started with the caveman or whoever picked up a stick and imagined the power that he held in his hand. What I do know is that the people who run the game don't want outside interference, and that makes the information you found potentially very dangerous, if you catch my meaning."

Gus and Pauline stare at him.

"Sir, if that is true, then isn't it more important that this cartel be stopped before we are all turned into mindless drones doing their bidding?"

"In theory, yes, that is correct, but I have seen what such people are capable of. They have no feelings or humanitarian views. It isn't about the money, per se, but more a matter of power. It is an addiction to control--the very essence of the human spirit. I'm not sure they even appreciate how far they have taken things."

"Then why don't we start our own cartel and neutralize them?"

The officer smiles. "What a great idea, except for the fact they hold all the cards. They have the power and machinery to fight us, not to mention the money. Whenever there's money to be made, 'Is this going to harm anyone?' is not usually the first question people ask. All that people want to know is, 'How much can I make?'"

Clearly the officer has come to embrace the cartel's viewpoint.

"Makes sense to me."

"Gus!" exclaims Pauline. "How can you say that? You know what those people are about."

Gus gives her a gentle kick under the table.

"I know, Pauline, but you heard what he said. They're holding all the cards. We might as well get what we can for ourselves."

The officer puts his hands on their shoulders. "I'll give you some time to make this decision. Call me at the office in the morning. Pauline, think carefully about what Gus is saying. He seems to have a good grasp of the situation. Let's get whatever we can to make ourselves comfortable until the next war." He turns and walks away.

"Gus, how the--"

"Not here and not now," says Gus. "We have a lot to talk about."

She pauses. Gus rarely speaks to her in such a way. The fact he is doing so now can only mean one thing. He has a plan.

Springtime means new life. The trees sport rich new leaves while flowers bloom like madness in the sun. Bees in search of nectar busily work the pollen from flower to flower. Forest creatures spend their days building nests. Bears wake from their long winter naps and are on the prowl for a meal. New life and new beginnings are daily themes. The fresh air is intoxicating, inviting every form of life to relax and put the long winter's harshness behind them. It is impossible not to give in to the overpowering sense of languorousness. Just find a tree with a patch of grass and forget all about your troubles.

The dirt road fans dust in every direction as the car draws closer to Gus and Pauline's summer cabin by the lake. Pauline stares out the window, her eyes drinking up the season. Gus is deep in thought, motoring the car as if on a mission. Pauline is jolted from her blissful reverie by a hard bump in the road.

"Hey, cowboy, watch the bumps. I almost lost my teeth."

"Sorry, honey. I was... distracted."

"Are you ready to tell me what's on your mind?"

"Let's get to the cabin and talk there... after a drink... or two... or three."

"Are we a little stressed?"

Gus finally can't help himself and smiles at her. "You can always make me smile even when it seems like there's nothing to smile about."

"Yeah, well, when we get to the cabin I will put a permanent smile on your face."

The car suddenly speeds up. "Is that a promise?"

"Absolutely. That is if you don't get us killed first."

He looks at her. "What's that supposed to mean?"

She looks through the windshield and points at something. Standing in the road a short distance in front of their car is a deer. Gus slams on the brakes and hits the horn. The deer looks up and sprints off into the woods. Gus slows down and looks over at Pauline and smiles.

"Let's get back to how you're going to put a smile on my face when we get to the cabin."

She playfully leans toward him. "Let's get there first and then I won't need words."

Smoke from the fireplace curls out of the chimney and swirls around the full moon, its light reflecting off the still waters of the lake. It is the perfect evening to enjoy an after-dinner drink on the porch swing.

"Okay, Gus, truth or consequences time."

"I have given it a lot of thought, and I think we should fight fire with fire."

Pauline looks at him with bated curiosity. "Okay, I'll bite. What exactly do you mean?"

"What I mean is that I think our friendly recruiting officer is part of this setup. If my hunch is correct, then the infiltration goes deep within the war department as well as our entire intelligence community. It means we have to do what we did during the war. We start with a small, trusted group of well-trained agents and build from there."

Pauline stands up and walks to the end of the porch. Gus waits for her to say something. But she simply stares at the lake. Gus goes over and puts his arm around her. She leans against him.

"It really is pretty, isn't it, Gus?"

"Yes. Peaceful, too."

The words sink in for both of them with a quiet reminder of a war that was still fresh in their minds. Memories of the horrors that mankind inflicted on its military and civilian populations will haunt them for the rest of their lives. The unthinkable acts of cruelty committed in the name of national interest by countries desperate to win the war only to reduce one another's country to rubble while breaking the spirit of its loyal and life-giving patriots. The victor gained but a moment in the sun, for the victory, when assessed through the lens of time, pointed to empty hands and families robbed of husbands, wives, fathers, mothers, sisters, and sons in lieu of tears and haunting thoughts of how it might have been to hug their loved ones once again.

Pauline's eyes fill with tears. "Maybe we should just get out altogether. We could live here and put the past behind us. I don't want you involved in something that takes you away and leaves me wondering if I will ever see you again. I need you now more than ever."

He takes her in his arms and holds her tightly. "I have never known you to want to give up. How am I supposed to forget what I know? What about all the people who will be affected by what this cartel is planning? How could I live with myself knowing I could have done something?"

Wiping the tears from her eyes, she says, "Come inside with me, I have a gift for you."

"A gift? We're in the middle of a conversation."

"It can wait."

Pauline takes his hand and leads him inside. The door closes, holding at bay the outside world and leaving them in the security of their cozy cabin. After sitting Gus in his favorite chair, she goes over and pulls a small, wrapped box from a brown paper bag and hands it to him. He looks at her and smiles.

"Now what could this possibly be? A new car? No. A suit? No. I give up... I guess I'll just have to open it." Slowly he opens the package. He looks inside the box, and then he looks up at her. She smiles. He is speechless. He looks inside the box again. He reaches in and carefully removes two hand-knitted booties. Pauline goes over and sits in his lap.

"Where do you stand on fatherhood?"

"I, um, well..."

The question was so ridiculous that they both start laughing.

"Shouldn't you have your feet up or something?"

"Or something." She gives him a sultry look and begins to undress him.

"Is it safe to… I mean, are you sure we won't hurt the, um…"

"I think the word you're looking for is 'baby.' And no, we cannot hurt the baby. Now stop fidgeting and take off your clothes before I rip them off."

The first rays of daylight are accompanied by the smell of freshly brewed coffee. Without opening his eyes Gus smiles. "I'm going to be a father… Daddy. Has a nice ring to it. I should go buy some sports gear today and…"

Pauline shouts from the kitchen, "Okay, lazy bones, up and at it."

"Already up, honey." He gets out of bed, puts on a terry cloth bathrobe and slippers, and heads toward the kitchen. Focusing his sleepy eyes he begins to laugh.

Pauline turns around and sees him standing there beholding the gastronomic bounty she has prepared.

He clears his throat. "Are we expecting company?"

She rubs her stomach. "Yes, now sit and eat."

They share a delicious, intimate meal, and afterwards Gus clears the dishes before joining Pauline.

With one look she knows what is on his mind. "Just come out and say it."

"Okay, here's the thing. I think we have to play this very carefully. First, we should call the recruiting officer. We will explain that since you are pregnant, we have decided not to accept his generous offer and that we are going into private practice. He shouldn't have a problem with that. The next thing is to contact Dave Peeplet at the War Department and recruit him. Then we can start to build our group and go after these bastards."

"I agree--under one condition."

Gus becomes uneasy. He knows her conditions are non-negotiable when she says it that way, but he thinks, *Why not give it a try?*

"Okay, what is the condition for discussion?"

"Nice try, Gus. This condition is not up for discussion." They smile at each other in a show of mutual respect.

"Okay, darling, let's hear it."

"I'm part of the team." Her voice was firm and left no room for discussion.

"And what about our baby?"

"He or she is still too young to take on a job of this magnitude. Gus, other families have two working parents."

"True, but most of them aren't planning a covert operation. Please reconsider."

"Okay, Gus, I will."

He smiles. "Really?"

"Yes, really." A brief moment passes. "Okay, I have reconsidered and the condition stands."

The smile fades from his face. He knows it is futile to discuss the matter any further. "It's a deal, but you work on the inside and not in the field."

"Of course. By the time we are operational I will be a full-time mother. Now, don't we have one more issue to resolve?"

"You mean where to hide the information I found on the mission?"

"Yes."

Gus goes over and rummages through his pack. "I had two small transparencies made of directions to the 'safe place' where the negatives and prints will be kept."

"Why two?"

"Actually the directions wouldn't all fit the size I had in mind."

Pauline is intrigued. "Where do we keep these directions--and who do we give them to in the event of our... demise?"

"I've been giving that some thought. The locket I gave you for our first anniversary would be the perfect place. We can slip them right behind our pictures. No one would ever think of looking there."

"And who do we trust with this locket? You realize that the minute we tell anyone about this secret it becomes compromised."

"Let's just say it will stay in the family for generations to come."

"What if both of us are killed?"

Gus shakes his head. "Then there would be nothing to prevent them from completing their sick plans. That cannot be an option."

Pauline removes the locket and hands it to Gus. He opens it and gazes at the pictures, one on each side, taken on their wedding day. He reflects on how quickly time passes and how young they both looked. Pauline goes over to him and sits on his lap, wrapping her arms around his neck.

"We were so young…"

"You haven't aged a day." She smiles at him and runs her hand through his hair.

They embrace lovingly, enjoying the quiet splendor of their mountain retreat. It will be a long time before they know such peacefulness again.

Later that afternoon Gus calls the recruiting officer and explains their position. The recruiting officer expresses his disappoint but is understanding. Next Gus prepares to call Dave Peeplet. With the phone in his hand he turns to Pauline.

"Once I make this call, we are committed. Are you sure you want to be a part of this?"

"As sure as I know I want to have your baby." Gus drinks in her glowing beauty. Again she knows what he is thinking, but this time she simply smiles.

"Now place that call to Dave. We need him, and time is wasting."

Gus dials the number. It rings several times before someone picks up.

"Private Lawrence here. How may I direct your call?"

"Dave Peeplet, please."

"One moment, sir. I will connect you."

As Gus is put through, Pauline opens the locket and gazes at it, praying the secret it houses will never see the light of day. Her thoughts go to her unborn child and the world into which it will be born. She knows their decision is the right one. They will just have to find ways to enjoy their life as parents. The consummate mother-to-be, she wants to protect her unborn baby from the dark side of humanity.

"Hello, this is Agent Peeplet. May I help you?" comes the voice on the other end of the line.

"Dave, this is Gus."

"Hey, Gus, how the hell are you?"

"I'm fine, Dave. How are things with you?"

"Really good. Listen, Dave, is there an afternoon this week we can sit down and talk?"

"What's on your mind?"

"I'd rather talk about it in person."

"Okay, buddy, whatever you say. How about Thursday at 12:30? We can chat over lunch."

"That would be perfect. Usual place?"

"You bet. And Gus?"

"Yes?"

"It's your meeting, so it's your treat. That includes dessert." This is followed by a chuckle.

"Deal. Oh, by the way, I have some great news. Pauline is pregnant."

"Hot stuff, daddio. Do you know who the father is?"

Gus laughs. "See you Thursday, you maniac."

The soda jerks are busy making malts for the high school kids sitting at the fountain listening to their favorite tunes playing on the miniature jukeboxes lining the counter. The green marbleized Formica stretches the length of the restaurant, with immaculately aligned stools covered in gray vinyl complete with spinning heads. While waiting for their drinks some of the kids show their impatience by spinning as fast as they can, trying to avoid being thrown off their suburban rodeo ride. It's good innocent fun. The winner of the game is required to walk ten feet or more, which always brings enormous laughter from the onlookers as the dizzy contestant wobbles along crookedly. The noise level is sky high, making it the perfect meeting place for Gus and Dave.

The waitress delivers luncheon specials to the tables, each white plate filled with enough food to feed an entire family. The rough napkins scour faces clean, the silverware is still hot from the dishwasher, and the wide-mouth Coke glasses are filled with ice and topped with a cherry. Every table in the place is a booth, complete with its own "five cents for two songs" jukebox. The floor-to-ceiling windows, overlooking the highway for half of the restaurant patrons, feature a spectacle of fast-moving cars. Speeding convertibles occupied by cheerleaders with long flowing hair and colorful pompoms are abundant. Across the highway is a new mall teeming with anxious shoppers in search of the perfect bargain. Unlike during the war, whose memory continues to recede, their lives seem comfortable and carefree.

"Here are your specials," says the waitress as she sets down two steaming plates of food. "Is there anything else I can get you?"

They both shake their heads.

"Okay, if you need me, just holler. The name is Janie."

"Thanks, Janie," they both reply as she heads to her next table.

Dave is the quintessential suit in that after you shake hands with him you feel somehow violated. Although he was once the epitome of physical fitness, he now shows signs of a pot belly, has gray hair, and is slightly hunched over.

"How's Pauline feeling?"

"Pretty good. The doctor said the first three months are the hardest, then it should ease up on her."

"You okay?"

"Just fine."

"What's on your mind that you couldn't talk about over the phone?"

"Pauline and I were approached by a recruiting officer."

"Sounds above board. What is the play?"

"Well…we never got that far. We bowed out since she is pregnant, and now we want to go private."

"Something tells me this is about something else altogether."

"Actually, it has to do with the documents I found on the mission."

"Oh, shit, Gus, why don't you leave it alone. If the agency says the papers are bogus, then what makes you think otherwise?"

"For one thing, I never told them the extent of the documents I found. There were other papers that showed a game plan that seems to have been followed to the letter during the war."

"But that was war time. This is peacetime. The two probably have nothing to do with each other."

"Not necessarily. Let's suppose that a cartel was formed during the war. And let's suppose that there were American industrialists and Nazis working together toward a larger goal."

"Such as?"

"Such as the real winner is the one who owns more power at the end of the war."

"What kind of power, Gus?"

"What if I told you that they have been experimenting with mind control through drugs and that they intended to use it to take over the entire world?"

"I would advise you to stop reading science-fiction."

"I know how it sounds, but I have the papers to prove it--and no one in the intelligence world will listen."

"Are you suggesting that everyone in our field is in on it?"

"No, not everyone, but a great many of the top players have a stake in it."

"Why? What would be their motivation?"

"Look at it this way. If the American industrialists, with their money and propaganda machine, joined forces with the Nazis, with their medical research and experiments, and were able to discover a way to enact mind control on a large scale, wouldn't that seem like a perfect match?"

"What you are suggesting is impossible in this day and age. The Nazis lost the war and we won, end of story. There are established rules in Germany about the Reich and the ability of that nation to ever form another Nazi party again."

"But what if they went private? Don't forget what Hitler said about his own people--that the way to control the masses is through physical and mental terror. If they really are developing mind-control drugs, there is no telling what this cartel is capable of achieving."

"Gus, let's assume you are right. Then what can we--or anyone for that matter--do? We don't have the men or the machinery to fight such an organized conspiracy. And that's assuming you are right, which I might add is a big assumption. And we all know what can happen when you make assumptions..."

"Which is why I think the first step is to form and train a team."

"It's not going to be easy keeping this team a secret, you know."

"So far it's only Pauline, you, and me."

Dave clears his throat. "Gus, you are a friend and I have tremendous respect for you, but I am not field trained. And honestly... this is something that scares the shit out of me. I have always been an inside man. Not to mention I enjoy the paycheck and benefits. Have you figured out how to fund this operation of yours?"

"Yes, but that's a story for another time. Are you saying that you don't want to help?"

"No, I am saying that I am not willing to give up my day job for a wild goose chase. I know how important this is to you, but frankly I think there are too many holes in your investigation."

"Dave, I haven't told you the whole story. Only Pauline and I know the full scope. I thought it would be better for everyone involved that they not have all the pieces. That way if we get infiltrated we can cut our losses and avoid jeopardizing the entire operation."

"Okay, Gus, here is what I am willing to do. You can count on me to help, but I cannot give up my position in the War Department. Besides, if you utilize me for research it will be more helpful to have someone on the inside accessing information that you are definitely going to need. Don't you think?"

"Actually, Dave, we could use an inside man. Pauline and I thought you might be the right guy for the job. So, is it settled?"

Dave reaches across the table and they shake hands. The first member of Gus's elite team is now in place.

"Excuse me," says the waitress, standing over the table watching the two men holding hands. "Are you guys finished or would you like some coffee and a cigarette?"

They smile uncomfortably as they separate hands. Dave looks at the waitress. "I'll have a cup of coffee, and since my date is paying for lunch, I would like to see the dessert menu, please. Oh, and since you offered, I will take that cigarette."

The waitress rolls her eyes and heads off. They both sit there for a moment, then start laughing the way the kids at the soda fountain are laughing. Gus is relieved to have the first big step behind him. The kids continue spinning and falling off the stools. The day has seen a momentous development, although only time will reveal the true scope of Dave's acceptance of Gus's invitation.

THREE

Gus, Pauline, and their son, Joe, now four years old, are playing in the living room of their two-bedroom apartment. Gus performs sleight-of-hand tricks, much to the delight of Joe. Pauline watches her husband and son together, cherishing the sound of their laughter.

"Hey, Joe, how about we make Mommy disappear?"

Joe appears concerned. "For always, Daddy?"

Gus laughs. "No, just for a little while."

Joe looks at his mother adoringly, thinking about the goodnight kisses she gives him so he can fall asleep at bedtime.

"Mom, will you promise to come back?"

"Wait a minute, you two. I don't remember anyone asking me if I wanted to disappear in the first place."

Joe goes over to her with his arms outstretched. "Please, Mommy, let Daddy make you disappear. He promises to bring you back."

Pauline eyes Gus with a suspicious squint and a smile on her face.

"Okay, but if Daddy forgets to bring me back you remind him of his promise, okay?"

"Okay, Mommy. I promise." He reaches around her neck with both arms and hugs her for dear life. Tears of joy fill Pauline's eyes.

"I wove you, Mommy."

"I wove you too, Honey."

Gus stands up holding a blanket. Joe sits in the front row, his eyes glued to his dad's every move. Although no one knows it at the time, what is about to unfold will create a childhood memory Joe will carry with him for the rest of his life. Joe sweeps the room with his eyes, absorbing every nuance of detail. Atop the old television positioned at the far end of the room is a bronze statue of cowboys and Indians. Next to the TV is a small rack in which magazines are neatly stacked. A TV Guide sits ceremoniously next to the statue. The television broadcasts images in black and white, painting the room with a flickering glow. The living room rug is thick and cozy. The pictures on the walls are the culmination of three generations, some of them faded with time. The sturdy wooden end tables support tall lamps with large shades. The curtains in the apartment are clean but fraying at the ends. The claw foot sofa holds two handmade pillows. The smell of dinner lingers in the air. The paint on the walls is peeling from years of coat after coat.

Gus looks at his son, and on the count of one... two... three... he drops the blanket to the floor. Pauline has vanished. Joe gasps with delight. He stands up and begins looking all around.

"She's not in there, Joe," says Gus. Joe looks at his dad, puzzled.

"I bet she is in the bathroom."

Gus steps over to the bathroom door and opens it slightly so Joe can peek inside, never revealing Pauline standing behind the door. Joe goes from the bathroom to his parents' bedroom and looks all around. Then he smiles at his dad, who is pointing under the bed. He drops to his knees and with a swift motion pulls aside the bed covers.

"Okay, Dad, you win."

Gus smiles at Joe. "Shall we bring her back?"

"We promised her we would."

"Let's go back into the family room and keep our promise then."

Joe jumps up and down ecstatically and runs back into the family room. As Gus passes the bathroom he whispers to Pauline, "Get ready..." She prepares to come out of the bathroom on his cue and hide behind the blanket that Gus will be holding up high.

"Dad, are you sure you can make Mommy come back?"

Gus smiles and says the magic words. He drops the blanket to reveal Pauline, who stands there with open arms to receive Joe.

"Mommy!" He runs over and hugs her tightly. While Gus answers a phone call, mother and son continue their loving embrace.

"Hello," says Gus.

"Hello, Gus. We have an opportunity," the voice says.

"Great, let's meet up in about an hour."

Without another word, the caller and Gus both hang up. Pauline shoots Gus a knowing look.

Gus gets his coat and picks up Joe. "You be a good boy for Daddy and take care of Mommy until I get home, okay?"

"Okay, daddy. I'll try to make Mommy disappear."

Gus laughs, and hugs and kisses his son goodnight. Pauline walks him to the door and they embrace warmly. "I hope this is what we have been waiting for," she says. "Five years is a long time to wait. We could use a break. Be careful, sweetheart."

Each time Gus leaves the apartment Pauline can't help wondering if she will ever see him again. Despite Gus's desire to keep her out of the operation, her comprehensive knowledge of the documents and their whereabouts makes this impossible. It also makes her a very vulnerable target. His only hope is that the cartel doesn't know what she knows.

Gus arrives at the meet location to find all the members of his team assembled.

Making his way to the podium, Gus says, "Please have a seat. We have a lot to go over." He clears his throat.

"Tonight we are finally going to make a difference in this cold war we are fighting. I have in my hand the time and location of the next cartel meeting. This comes to us compliments of a friend from the intelligence community. It's known that the full ten-member board will be present at this meeting. And despite the fact we weren't invited, we'll be there, too, locked and loaded. There will be no prisoners. We will need a clean-up team to make sure there isn't a single trace that they were ever there. Please open your packets and let's begin. We have two days before the mission."

The meeting goes into the night and shows no signs of slowing. Coffee, sandwiches, and donuts are consumed by the truckload. Each man is assigned a specific function. They must time their moves precisely or a domino effect will take place costing them the mission and possibly their lives.

Their concentration is broken by the first rays of dawn peeking through the curtains and spotlighting the drawing sprawled across the conference table. Gus looks up and reads the exhausted looks of everyone there.

"I think we have done enough for tonight. We will meet again tomorrow to finalize the plans. At that time each of you will be given the time and place to meet for the mission. Now go home and get some sleep. You all look like shit."

The others smile and disperse, all of them going in different directions in an attempt to avoid bringing any unnecessary attention to the group.

Gus arrives home just as the sun clears the horizon. Pauline is asleep on the couch. She waited up for him until four o'clock, when sleep finally claimed her. Gus kneels down beside her and strokes her hair. He kisses her forehead.

"I love you."

"I love you, too," she mumbles, surprising him. "And if you ever, ever scare me like that again by not calling, I will kill you myself."

He knows better than to argue with her. "I promise I won't let it happen again." Then he teases, "But you should have seen the bowling scores last night."

She rolls over to face Gus and punches him on the arm. A wrestling match ensues, and it soon ends in laughter.

"I'll give you bowling scores."

He musters his best John Wayne voice. "So, ya wanna play rough?"

"Now just calm down... Don't even think of..."

Too late. He is on top of her tickling her mercilessly. Every muscle in her face is tightly wrapped around the laughter. She frees her arm only to be restrained again. This goes on until they both lay side by side, laughing and exhausted.

"I needed that. The guys all say hi and asked about Joe."

"When is the mission?"

"This Friday. You'll have to arrange a sitter."

"You mean call your mother!"

"Well, yes, it is free that way."

"And Joe always has a blast--candy, ice cream, and too much television."

"Sounds great."

"Sort of."

The next day is spent briefing the team members for the last time before deployment. Every man is fully focused on his specific function and the success of the mission. Their confidence in one another fuels their belief the mission will succeed brilliantly. There are only twelve hours left before history will begin rewriting itself.

Shadows dance on the floor as they pierce through the sheers and continue into the apartment. The moon is so bright it looks like daytime. Pauline, Gus, Joe, and Grandma sit quietly watching television. Joe is engrossed in his favorite cartoon, munching on popcorn.

In a low voice so Joe won't hear, Grandma asks, "So, where are you taking Pauline tomorrow? I hope it is a good restaurant."

"Of course, Mom. I always take her to a good restaurant, just not an expensive one."

Pauline flutters her eyelids. "You are so my knight in shining armor. I don't care where we eat as long as we are together."

"Watch out, Mom, I think she's going to blow."

Joe's show is over, and he begins campaigning for ice cream.

"Come with me." Grandma extends her hand and walks him into the kitchen.

"I am glad your mom came over tonight. He adores her."

"Yeah, it is nice to see. Is everything set on your end for tomorrow evening?"

"All set. We were having some trouble with the earpieces, but that's been resolved."

"Good. I hope we will finally be able to convince someone in the intelligence community that this is a real threat."

"For the sake of all of us, I hope so, too."

Friday evening for most people means the beginning of a weekend without work or responsibility, to shut off their work minds, and looking forward to play time. A time to partake of a little harmless self-indulgence and mindless frivolity. It is an excellent opportunity to put a mission into the go mode unnoticed.

The team has assembled. The mood is somber, with each person singularly focused on getting the job done. The next few hours could prove historic. The plan has been dissected and thought through ad nauseam, and every conceivable detail is timed to the accuracy of the finest Swiss watch money can buy. Each person will enter the building in a different way, with everyone heading to the top floor. Where things get problematic is gaining entrance into the building without raising any red flags within the cartel's security force.

"Okay, everybody, you know the drill. Let's do this thing."

Each person takes a duffel bag and leaves the room. Gus goes over to Pauline. "Stay in touch."

"Gus, you are now twelve seconds behind." Then she grabs him and pulls him so their lips all but meet. "See you later... and we can finish that kiss."

"Excellent technique in motivation."

"Twenty-two seconds behind schedule."

"I'm going already." Gus grabs his duffel bag and heads out the door.

The high rise is bathed in the glow of the full moon. Each of the large glass panels on the southwest side of the towering building throws back a bright image, making it look like there are dozens of colorful harvest moons. The smattering of clouds in the night sky imparts a surreal three-dimensionality.

Throughout the city it seems like an ordinary night, with minimal traffic and a few pedestrians strolling along the well-maintained sidewalks. A sewer cover is quickly removed and one of the team members enters the open hole and then turns on his headlamp. He stops and reaches up to slide the cover back over the hole. He descends the cold wrought iron rungs, places the duffel bag on the ground, unzips it, removes his earpiece from its protective case.

Placing it in his ear, he says, "Base, this is number four, can you read me?"

"Copy that. Loud and clear, number four," replies Pauline.

"Anyone else on yet?" There is an unnerving pause. She looks at her watch. Come on, Gus, answer me.

"Base, this is number two."

"Copy that."

Another eternity passes, although it is still within the mission's tolerance timetable.

"Number three here."

"Copy."

There is another long pause. Pauline is becoming increasingly concerned.

"Number one here."

She breathes a sigh of relief. "Nice to hear from you, number one. Okay, we will keep this channel hot until you are clear of the building. You know the drill. From here on out, no extraneous chatter. Go silent unless there is a problem. Check your watches. On my mark. Ready... mark!"

With that command, she settles in for an evening of silence. Pauline feels very much alone and wishes more than ever she were a field operative. She reaches into her pocket and takes out a photo, staring at it with love. In the picture Joe is holding a horseshoe crab and has a huge smile on his face. She removes the unisex locket from around her neck and looks at it. The silver is tarnished from years of opening it to look at the photo within of the happy couple on their wedding day. The information that is now embedded behind the picture makes it even more special to her. She has prayed every night for the last five years that it will never have to be used.

"Base, this is number four. We have two additional hostiles."

"Hold your position, number four. Number one, do you copy?"

"Yes."

"We have two unaccounted hostiles."

"Have them removed."

"Number four, you are cleared to remove obstacles."

"Copy that."

Number four puts down his bag and threads a silencer onto his firearm. Cautiously he walks up the stairs, a jacket draped over one arm. The hostiles are one flight of stairs above him. He approaches the two men, who are engaged in a conversation with each other, and clears his throat. Both men react with drawn weapons. Number four drops to his knees.

"Please don't shoot," he screams. "You can have my money. I have a wife and two children."

One of the guards holsters his weapon and walks over to number four.

"Relax, mister. You just startled us. Here, let me help you up."

As the man reaches out, number four grabs his hand and pulls the man past him, sending him head over heels down the metal stairs. The distraction gives number four enough time to shoot the other guard between the eyes. As the man slides down the bloodstained door, number four turns to the man lying at the base of the stairs, and in a single motion he launches a knife at him, severing the man's vocal cords, preventing him from screaming. The man clutches his neck in hopeless desperation, blood spurting between his fingers. He falls to the floor with eyes wide as death closes in on him.

"Base, the two hostiles have been removed."

"Listen up, team. You are cleared to proceed."

The team moves into their positions. Each second is precious yet moves at glacier speed. Adrenaline floods their systems, urging them toward their goal. With only thirty seconds to spare, they are ready. Pauline watches the seconds tick away. She is the one who must ultimately issue the call to action.

"Thirty seconds. Number one?"

"Ready."

"Number two?"

"All set."

"Number three?"

"One second." Pauline hears the man struggling with something. "Okay, got it."

She continues. "Number four?"

"Locked and loaded."

"Okay, fifteen seconds. I will start the count at ten. You go on 'now'."

No one says a word as they commit mentally to action mode. Every member's alert level tops out at the highest level since training began years ago. The wait for the final countdown seems like an eternity.

Finally, Pauline's authoritative voice comes through their earpieces. "Ten... nine... eight... seven... six... five... four... three... two... one... NOW!"

The man on the roof jumps off, trailing his rope. If he is slightly off, he will swing into the side of the building instead of the glass window. Agent number two opens the fire door and shoots both guards standing watch outside the penthouse door. They fall to the floor dead without ever knowing what hit them.

Inside the room, the cartel meeting is underway. Cuban cigars and the finest cognacs are in no short supply. The place is infused with a celebratory feeling because they are close to a breakthrough in their enterprise. The wealth in the room is obvious, from the expensive hand-tailored material of every suit to the ruby stickpin tie clasps. Rolex watches adorn wrists and diamond rings catch the light and fling it back opulently. The shoes are all imported from the best shoemaker in Italy. Titanium briefcases line the floor. Freshly starched linen tablecloths cover the marble surfaces, preventing the fine bone china and baccarat crystal from making a sound. Each imported chair is hand-carved and covered in the finest antique floral silk Damask fabric. Champagne flutes are filled with a rare vintage of Dom Perignon. The silverware that finishes the table, from Louis XVI's personal collection, is highlighted with 22-carat gold trim. Rare eclectic antique furniture that would be the pride of any museum collection fills the room, giving it an Old-World feel. The art on the walls consists of original works by the world's most celebrated painters, including Monet, Renoir, Picasso, Van Gough, and Dali.

It is, simply put, a dream setting, and every bit of it had been looted by the Nazis during the war from the slaughtered Jews.

Outside the room and along the top of the glass window a shadow appears as the rope grows taut. Holding onto the rope with one hand and a machine gun with the other, the agent swings toward the pane of glass. He opens fire, shattering the glass and sending the men inside the room into absolute panic. At that same instant, the front door crashes open, the wall vent flies off, and the adjoining door to the next suit is caved in. Each team member unleashes a death sentence from a different entrance. The cartel members scramble for cover as the room becomes engulfed in ricocheting bullets ripping through anything in their path. The stuffing from the chairs and couches explodes outward until the room resembles the interior of a snow globe. The baccarat crystal shatters into projectile shards ripping through paintings and tearing the tablecloth into worthless shreds and marring the marble surface beyond repair. The silverware resonates at different pitches, adding to the confusion and chaos of Old-World charm colliding with New World violence in a harsh enactment of survival of the fittest.

One of the cartel members reaches for a handgun, but before he can get it out of the holster two agents turn their attention to him. The armor-piercing bullets go through him one at a time, causing the body to jerk up and down from the impact. The finely tailored suit is now drenched in blood as his limp and broken body falls to the floor. Another cartel member makes a break for it from behind one of the couches. The rope from the agent that crashed through the glass pane trips the man, throwing him off balance, and he falls out the window. His screams of fear are so loud they can be heard above the gunfire. All the cartel members lie dead as the din of death and destruction diminishes to a chorus of echoes.

Gus rapidly surveys the room.

"Shit, there are only six bodies here. There was supposed to be ten. Base, this is number one. We are finished here and using the escape plan."

"Okay, number one, clean-up team's ETA is less than a minute. We will rendezvous in eleven minutes."

Gus turns to his team. "Let's get out of here before the police show up."

They leave as the last few tufts of furniture stuffing are still settling gently to the floor. Peace and quiet return to the room as the team makes its way to the rendezvous point.

FOUR

A newspaper is neatly folded and placed next to an espresso cup. Near the cup rests a spoon, and next to that a single sugar cube and lemon peel. The ornate silver spoon is highly polished, sending out a blinding pinpoint shard of light from its center. The glass tabletop reflects the leaves from the overhanging tree as the wind gently stirs the music from them. Baby tears accent the single-stem rose sprouting from a baccarat crystal vase.

A hand slowly picks up the sugar cube, setting it gingerly on the spoon before delicately submerging it in the hot coffee. The cube melts, releasing its sweetness into the bitter espresso. The lemon peel is bent in half to massage the rim of the cup. The spoon is stirred in a counterclockwise motion. Five ceremonious stirs and the spoon is withdrawn from the espresso. After two delicate taps on the rim of the cup, it is carefully returned to its place.

A breakfast tray arrives consisting of a croissant and fresh fruit. The first delectable sip of espresso explodes on his taste buds. Guava juice accents the other flavors of the continental breakfast. One last sip of coffee and the phone is picked up and dialed. The phone rings twice on the other end.

"We seem to have a problem," says the man eating his breakfast. His voice is serious but encouraging and in total control.

"Yes," said the voice on the other end. "It seems six of our board members are gone."

"Not to worry. Our sources said this might occur."

"You knew about this?"

"Of course. That is why four of us are still alive."

"I don't understand!"

"I wasn't sure if the American intelligence could be fully trusted. Now I am confident. The loss was necessary for our purpose to survive. It is part of the game we play."

"What next?"

"We now know who targeted our operation. It is time to retaliate and end their organization. We will meet in two days in Geneva, and I will set out the plan. When this minor disruption is behind us we will move with absolute certainty towards success. Call the others and tell them to meet at our mountain chalet."

"Very well."

The call is ended. The neatly folded newspaper is systematically opened. The headlines read, Mafia War Continues. No Bodies Discovered. Police Baffled.

The phone is picked up and dialed again. "Hello, I would like to speak with Dave, please." After a short wait a voice on the other end of the phone comes on.

"Hello, this is Dave Peeplet. May I help you?"

"Your information was reliable and very valuable. You will be duly rewarded." The phone is hung up and the remaining breakfast is consumed.

Dave hangs up, untroubled by guilt for having played both ends of the intelligence espionage game. He is perfectly positioned in the War Department to selectively leak information at a "reasonable cost." He thinks to himself, *after all, I never thought of myself as greedy, just entrepreneurial.*

The way he sees it, it is just the cost of doing business. If he didn't do it, then someone else would. Dave wants money and he doesn't care how he gets it. He wants the power and prestige that wealth affords him. Besides, he is a family man and has to look after his own. Who could blame him for that? Still, a small part of him wonders if the cartel will keep their word not to harm Gus or his family.

Reflected in the lake are the snow-capped mountaintops of Geneva. Sailboats and powerboats enter and leave this quiet place of endless relaxation. Geneva is a living dichotomy. During wartime it remained neutral. During times of peace, war criminals sought safe haven there. The cartel's chalet, snuggled in a dense region of the Swiss Alps, is protected by electronic surveillance and heavily armed guards.

The tall steel gates swing open as a stretch limousine cruises into the secured compound. As the limousine reaches the front entrance, one of the guards walks over to the car and promptly opens the door with military stiffness. The four-member cartel exits the vehicle and is met with customary salutations.

"Heil Hitler!"

Each member responds with salutes.

Inside the chalet, at the rear of the conference room, is a breathtaking view. The conference table is made from pure ivory inlaid with gold. The base holding the tabletop is molded from titanium. The chairs are upholstered with the finest handcrafted leather. The chalet is constructed from the rarest woods, accented with tiger wood from Africa.

The remaining cartel members enter the room and take their seats. The meeting gets underway.

"We are gathered here today to discuss a number of topics. We need to address our long-term goals and implementation of those goals. We also need to reach a decision on the little problem we recently experienced."

One of the other members interrupts. "There doesn't seem to be much to discuss. It is obvious that they must be eradicated."

The other two members agree enthusiastically.

"I agree, gentlemen, clearly this is what must be done. But we need to decide precisely how to do it and what benefits we can achieve along the way. If I may, it appears we have an opportunity to send a message to some of our associates and moles that any interference will be harshly dealt with." He turns to his assistant. "Have you the names and addresses?"

"Yes, sir." He hands him a piece of paper.

"I have here the names of the living dead. Within three days there will no longer exist any threat to our organization... or us."

He turns and hands the paper to his assistant. "Have the Aucht team assembled for this assignment."

"Any instructions, sir?"

"Yes, I want it done simultaneously so there can be no warning the others. Remind the team we do not tolerate failure."

"Yes, sir."

"Now, gentlemen, it has been a long trip. I want to suggest a glass of champagne to celebrate the removal of this minor obstacle. Then after a short rest we can discuss the rest of our itinerary."

Champagne is poured, and the men drink in quiet confidence that Gus and his team will soon be dead.

The doorbell rings. Joe jumps up from watching television and runs to the front door.

"Mom, can I open it, please oh please oh please?"

From the kitchen comes, "All right, honey, you can see who it is."

Joe reaches up, straining to reach the lock. He stands on his tiptoes with every muscle in his legs stretched to its full extent. His arms start to quiver from the effort. His fingertips barely brush against the wing-nut lock, occasionally slipping off. Hiking up his pants like a fighter ready to do battle, he squints his eyes with determination and with one last surge of effort he manages to wrap his little fingers around the lock, twisting it to the open position. Flattening out on his feet, he grips the doorknob with both hands and turns it. The door eases open.

Proud of his accomplishment, Joe smiles from ear to ear. His hair hangs lank before his eyes, a lollipop swirling in his mouth, and his trusty homemade slingshot peeks out of his back pocket. His shirt and shorts are freshly ironed. He is squeaky clean from his morning bath and has been anxiously awaiting the day's adventure. The large door swings open, and he takes a step backward to see who it is.

The area is brightly lit from the large window at the end of the hall, so Joe can only see a silhouette. The figure grasps an object, holding it across the stomach. A voice says, "This is for you, Joe."

Joe screams. His mother stops dead in her tracks in the kitchen and bolts to his aid.

"Mom, it's Grandma."

Pauline's stiffened body relaxes.

Grandma hands Joe a bag. "Here, Honey. Tell me if you like it."

He yanks open the bag before the door even has a chance to close. Pauline comes over to greet Gus's mom.

"Come on in. That is if you can scoot past Joe." Pauline turns her attention to Joe. "Honey, take that into the living room so Grandma can come in."

Joe takes the bag into the living room, where he soon lets out a series of happy screams.

"Mom, look, a bow and arrow set just like the one on TV!"

Before Pauline can say a word, Grandma cuts her off at the pass. "It has rubber tips, and the string is very loosely strung."

Pauline smiles. "That was very thoughtful. It will help keep him busy. Would you like some coffee and a piece of cake?"

"I thought you would never ask."

They sit enjoying coffee and crumb cake, watching Joe play cowboys and Indians. From the sounds he is making it would seem like Custer's last stand was in full swing.

"You know, I was thinking that you and Gus haven't been alone for an entire evening in about four years."

"It is tough, but we are managing."

"Managing... schmanaging. You two need to be together. Look, here is the deal. With your approval, I would like to take Joe with me today and have him spend the night. In the morning we can all meet and have breakfast together. What do you think?"

Pauline is not sure how she feels about being without her son for the entire night.

"What if he gets scared?"

"I have a phone. And it's not like he will be in another state or anything. How about if we ask Joe?"

"That sounds like a good start. But even if he says yes, I still have a problem."

"And that is?"

"What do I do alone with Gus?"

Grandma shoots her a look. "I am sure something will come up."

Pauline laughs. "Why, Mom!"

"I didn't mean that, but it's not a bad idea, you know."

"Mom!"

"Okay, Pauline, let's ask Joe. You work out the other thing with Gus."

"Joe, can you come here for a minute, please?"

"Sure, Grandma."

Joe enters the kitchen armed with his bow and arrow. "Which squaw wants talkum to chief?"

Pauline decides to play along. "Mom squaw here. Grandma squaw wants to take big chief on day trip and overnight at her teepee. What does chief say?"

Chief thinks about it. "Okay, I go with Grandma squaw if ice cream part of deal."

The two women look at each other.

"Your son learns fast."

"I wonder what side of the family he gets that from."

Grandma decides to change the subject. "Chief need clothes for overnight. You needum help packing horse, chief?"

"Yes, please... I mean, yes, squaw."

Joe and his grandma head into his room and pack some things for the trip. They return with a duffel bag filled with toys and clothes. Pauline laughs.

"That seems like a lot of stuff for an overnighter."

"Mom, I need this stuff. What if Grandma gets bored?"

Pauline thinks better of trying to convince him otherwise. "Well, chief, that is very thoughtful. You be a good Indian and listen to Grandma, okay?"

"Okay, Mom."

"How about a pinky swear."

They do the pinky swear, then they hug and kiss.

"The chief and I will meet you and big chief for breakfast in the morning. And stop worrying--he will be fine."

"It isn't him I am worried about." And with that she kisses her mother-in-law and son goodbye.

Trying to calm her one more time, Grandma says, "You'll be fine. Go out to dinner and a movie. Relax and enjoy the evening."

"Thanks."

Grandma and Joe leave the apartment, bound for an adventure of exploration and ice cream.

Gus and Pauline are sitting at a romantic table in the corner of their favorite restaurant. The dark wood paneling imparts a welcoming sense of warmth. Starched white tablecloths accent the simple elegance of the place. The beveled mirrors make the place look three times larger than it actually is. Each table is adorned with freshly cut flowers floating in a bowl of colored water. The napkins fan across the plates like proud peacocks. Soft music sets the mood for intimate conversation. The restaurant is known for staging a quiet romantic evening flavored with aromas from the kitchen to awaken even the most finicky diner's appetite. The longer you are there the greater your anticipation of an unforgettable meal. Putting the final touches on the scenario are two tall white candles flickering as Gus and Pauline enjoy some red wine and conversation.

"You know, looking at you in this light... It's like I'm falling in love with you all over again."

"And you look dashing in a tie and jacket."

They join hands across the table. Pauline slips off her shoe and runs her foot up Gus's leg. He looks at her and raises an eyebrow.

"Do I know you well enough for you to do that?"

"I think so. It kind of feels like a first date, doesn't it?"

"Ah, no, and I am glad it isn't."

"And why is that?"

"Well, for one thing, I wouldn't have had the pleasure of knowing you for so long and looking forward to the years ahead. Instead, all I would be thinking about is how to get you into bed."

"Any plans now?"

"Do I need one?"

"Of course. This is a date, after all."

Gus and Pauline sit talking for several hours, savoring their dinner and each other's company. They reminisce about all the wonderful times they have had, and they talk about Joe and about how much he has brought to their lives. Gus considers how beautiful his wife looks after all these years, while Pauline feels grateful for having married such a wonderful man. Gus and Pauline look into each other's eyes and smile, the crow's feet commemorating the joys of marriage and the long journey they have endured together.

"Excuse me," says the waiter. "I'm sorry to interrupt, but will there be any dessert or coffee this evening?"

They answer simultaneously, "Absolutely."

The waiter hands them the dessert menu. A quick glance passes between them and the orders fly.

"I'll have the crème brûlée."

"And for the gentleman?"

"Hot apple pie and ice cream. And two cups of regular coffee, please."

"Very good. I'll have that right out for you." He replaces their candles with a fresh pair and leaves.

"Gus, I have a question. With only a few of the cartel members still alive, do you think it is over?"

"Hard to say. Unfortunately, we aren't sure how much they have developed or who actually runs things. It could be the organization is like a lizard-- you grab the tail and it falls off only to grow again."

"Such poetry."

"Seriously, I wish it was over. The real problem is that as long as there are people on this earth, this kind of sick thinking will continue. It is the classic battle of Good vs. Evil, and the sad truth is there is an unlimited cast of evil players."

"How did we get to be the gatekeepers? Can't we just hand the baton over to the new generation?"

"Do I detect a 'desire to retire' speech?"

"No, you detect an 'I want to live some semblance of a normal life' speech. You know, a regular paycheck, white picket fence, all that stuff. And a dog."

"A dog? Where did that come from?"

"Your son."

"Uh-oh. You know we can't have a dog in the apartment."

"That is exactly my point. We need a house to raise our family. And I think I want another child. But this life we are living isn't conducive to a family."

"Rewind, please... Another child? You aren't... I mean, are you going to hand me another pair of knitted booties?"

"No, but tonight we can start to knit."

"Honey, I haven't told you the entire story behind the information I found."

"What does that mean?"

"Well, it means... Actually, it seems almost ridiculous, so I decided to see how things unfolded and then make my decision based on more information."

"And now?"

"Now it doesn't seem so ridiculous."

The waiter arrives and sets the coffee and dessert on the table. "Will there be anything else?"

"When you have a second we will take the check."

"Right away, sir."

"Pauline, let's enjoy the rest of tonight, and in the morning, I will lay out the entire scope of what I found."

"Okay, but if you leave out one detail, I will personally pull your toenails out one at a time. Deal?"

"You're tough, but deal. Eat fast--my knitting needle has a date."

While Gus and Pauline enjoy their dinner, masked men with silencers are rendezvousing with their targets. Each gunman holds a picture of the person he has been assigned to terminate. Some of the terminations include the wife because the cartel has no way of knowing how much confidential information a target might have shared with his spouse. Tonight has been designed to clean the slate thoroughly.

Each team enters its target's house. One by one the teams begin to eliminate anything alive. Silent bullets find their targets as blood flows from warm bodies, the fallen pleading for the lives of children and wives. The terrified cries of small voices calling for their mommy and daddy end in silence, with dolls and other toys covered in the blood of the innocent. Even the family dogs aren't spared. Any report to the cartel that anything was left alive means a sure death sentence to the team member responsible. Once the assassins complete their assignments, Gus and Pauline's elite team will have been wiped off the face of the earth.

Gus and Pauline stroll along the street holding hands and silently renew their vows. They squeeze each other's hand, feeling the warmth of anticipation that will consume them both in relaxed lovemaking the minute they arrive home.

"Gus."

"Yes, dear?"

"I can't help feeling like I'm back in high school."

"Meaning?"

"I've had butterflies in my stomach since we left the restaurant. I haven't felt like that since we first started dating."

"I know exactly what you mean--except I've had them for the past few hours."

"I almost forgot what it was like, just the two of us on a date. Things finally seem to be going right for us."

"You mean the mission?"

"Yes. That and the wonderful evening with the man I love."

"I love you, too, darling."

As they turn the corner leading to their apartment, they feel euphoric, knowing they have made a difference in an indifferent world. Ahead of them stretches an entire evening free from responsibility. It promises to be an evening to remember.

Gus unlocks the door to their apartment, but before Pauline can enter he stops her.

"Come here, you beautiful woman." He pulls her to him and kisses her passionately. Bending down, he hoists her up and carries her across the threshold.

"Careful of your back, Gus. You're not as young as you used to be."

"Have no fear, my dear."

They enter the apartment and close the door behind, locking it before proceeding. He carries her to the bedroom and puts her down.

"How about a nightcap?"

"Sounds wonderful." She turns to Gus wearing a seductive smile.

Gus drinks in her beauty. His body goes rigid and he looks confused.

"Gus, are you all right?"

He is unable to speak. The front of his shirt blossoms with bright red. Pauline is about to scream when bullets hit her several times in the chest. More bullets penetrate Gus's body. Their eyes lock as the life drains from their bodies. In that brief moment they issue each other a silent goodbye. Their thoughts are tortured, wondering what will become of their son. Who will love him like only they can? Who will take him to his ballgames? Who will teach him to be strong? Who will kiss him goodnight? Who will be there when he is lonely for Mommy or Daddy? Who will he snuggle next to during lightning storms? Who will hold him because they want him to know he is loved and special? Who will say, "I love you, Joe"?

Clinging desperately to the fraying threads of life, they fall to the floor. Their blood-soaked hands reach out, shaking from trauma, to touch each other for the last time. Draping from Pauline's neck is the locket, now filled with secrets. One of the assassins notices the trinket, reaches down, and yanks it roughly off her still body. The other assassin lowers his gun to Gus's head and pumps two bullets into his skull. The force separates their hands.

There is a knock at the front door. The assassins hasten silently to the broken window in the bedroom through which they entered and leave. Both bodies lie still in a pool of blood. Gasps come from Pauline's body as her chest rises and falls repeatedly.

The next day is mayhem for the homicide division as the detectives try desperately to piece together how such a rash of murders could have been committed at approximately the same time. The killings are front page news, as are the facts there are no clues or motive and many questions about who could have committed such an atrocity. Speculation points to gang violence, but the victims weren't part of any known crime circle. Other speculation points to occult retribution for the war. The frenzy of theories becomes tiresome. Ultimately the cases are closed and labeled "Unsolved."

Private burials are held for the surviving families. Joe's grandmother does not take him to the funeral. He already cried for his parents for a week, venting the first waves of pain and making way for the feelings of abandonment he will contend with for the rest of his life.

A few weeks later Joe and Grandma have settled into living with each other, but it is still very raw for them.

"Wake up, Joe. Time for school."

"I don't want to go to school, Grandma."

"Joe, you have to go. What else will you do?"

"I don't know. I just don't like anybody at school."

Joe's grandmother knows better. She goes over and sits on the edge of his bed, rubbing his back. Joe pulls the covers over his head but doesn't move away from her soothing touch.

"Come on, I have a bath ready for you. You always feel better after your morning bath."

Reluctantly he says, "Okay, Grandma. What's for breakfast?"

"What would you like?"

"How about that egg thing you make. You know, where you cut a hole in the middle and then put the egg in it."

"If that is what you want, then that is what you will have."

After his bath, Joe climbs onto the footlocker where his grandmother dresses him. She is getting on in years and her arthritis acts up more and more, although she never lets on that anything hurts. She maintains a cheerful demeanor to help conceal the unspeakable sadness she feels for the loss for her son and daughter-in-law.

"Grandma, tell me again why Mommy and Daddy had to die?"

Holding back her tears, she says, "Well, Honey, sometimes God needs people more than we do."

"How could he need them more than me?"

"Well, sometimes he has very special needs that we don't understand."

"I miss Mommy and Daddy," he says as tears roll down his face.

"So do I, Sweetheart. So do I."

"I hate God."

"Joe, you mustn't say that."

Through the tears he screams, "I HATE GOD, I HATE GOD, I WANT MY MOMMY AND DADDY."

Crying hysterically, he jumps off the footlocker and runs into his bedroom, slamming the door behind him. It is more than his grandmother can take. She slides down the wall onto the floor and weeps. Her sorrow becomes a full-blown emotional purge as she buries her face in her hands. All answers elude her, and she has no idea what to do next.

FIVE

The school bell rings, and doors fly open as screaming kids pour happily onto the playground for recess. The boys all gather in a group while the girls gather at their usual spot.

Christina stands with perfect posture, her long blond hair falling in two perfect braids past her shoulders to her waist. Her blue eyes are the first thing to grab your attention—until she smiles her devastating smile. Her girlfriends Amy, Laura, Michelle, and Sandra stand with her.

"What are you all looking at now?" asks Christina.

"Those boys over there," says Sandra. "I am so tired of them always saying they can beat us at everything. They are so annoying."

Michelle chimes in. "I wish we could challenge them to something that would shut them up or at least even the playing field."

"Yeah, me, too. But what can we do better than them?" Laura added.

Amy thinks for a moment. "It should be something that will really teach them a lesson. Christina, what do you think?"

"Well, they love playing with those stupid marbles of theirs. How about if we come up with a challenge about their large marbles they call 'shooters'?"

The other girls like the sound of it, but no one is sure how to go about it. Christina is already hatching a plot. She knows that it has to be a smooth operation so the boys will not figure it out until it is too late.

"Okay, girls, gather round and listen up."

She explains her idea in great detail. Wearing conspiratorial smiles, the girls walk over to the boys to goad them into the challenge. Christina leads the way. As they walk across the playground, the boys notice them coming.

Randy, Michael, Jack, Karl, and Jeff--the most popular boys in the class--all play sports together and form a tight band of comrades. They all live within three miles of one another and spend much of their free time trading baseball cards and riding bicycles in the woods. Each boy keeps half-filled balloons wrapped around his bicycle wheel frame, with each passing spoke making more noise than the one before. The neighbors always know how close they are from the noise level. They are an innocent rat pack whose members will become lifelong friends, staying in touch even after they go their separate ways to different colleges. They make a blood brother vow to get together once a year to catch one another up and for some good old rabble-rousing.

"Look sharp, guys," Michael says. "Christina and her friends at eleven o'clock and closing."

The boys laugh at his humor. The gap closes and the two groups face off.

"What's up, boys?" Christina asks with a smile.

"Just hanging around. What are you all up to?" says Michael.

Christina knows he likes her but will never admit it to the other boys.

Karl looks at the other girls, who look a bit scared. "You know, Christina, we hang out together as guys, you know, to do guy things."

"Karl, you have a real way with words. I guess that comes from repeating sixth grade three times."

Everyone responds with ooh and ahs. Karl is embarrassed and lacks a comeback, even though it is not true. Jeff comes to his friend's aid.

"Is that a new dress, Christina?

She smiles. "Yes."

"Didn't it come in your size?"

More ooh and ahs.

Christina goes on the offensive. "Cute, Jeff, I can see why you all hang out together. Listen, we have a challenge for you young men. That is if you're up for taking on a bunch of girls."

Jack laughs. "A challenge? From you? We don't play with dolls."

"How about a challenge that even you could do? Oh, wait--it requires thinking... Sorry, Jack."

Christina turns to leave. The other girls exchange confused looks and then start to follow her.

Jack takes the bait. "Hold on. Let's hear this big idea of yours.

Without hesitation Christina turns and walks confidently over to the boys.

"Okay, here is the deal. Today is Tuesday. On Thursday, we meet back here and see who has the best shooters."

Randy eyes her skeptically. "And the winner gets what?"

"How about the losers have to wear a sign on their back all-day Friday that says 'I'M A LOSER'."

"I didn't think you even knew what a shooter was," Jack says, full of himself.

She ignores Jack's comment. "Do we have a deal? Or are you big boys afraid of losing to some girls?"

The guys look at one another and then at her. Michael is given the nod from the others.

"You got a challenge. Now I think you girls should go home and start making those signs for your backs. And make sure the letters are nice and big."

The boys start laughing. The girls smile cutely back at them, and as they turn and walk away, Amy whispers something to the others.

"Wow, that went well. I just hope Christina's idea works or else I'm playing hooky on Friday."

The girls share a giggle and then set about doing their assigned chores.

Mrs. Randolph answers a knock at the door.

"Hello, Christina."

Christina smiles back at her. "Hello, Mrs. Randolph."

"Michael isn't here, dear. He is out playing with his friends and I don't expect him back until dinner. Did he know you were coming over here?"

"I actually came to talk to you, Mrs. Randolph. You see, it's about the marbles the boys in school play with."

"Oh, dear, don't I know. I almost fell down the stairs this morning when I stepped on one of those big ones. Michael called it a shootster."

"You mean a shooter."

"Why, yes. Don't tell me you play with those silly things?"

"No, but I want to learn, and I thought Michael would be willing to lend me his."

"Well, Michael is always talking about you."

Christina is surprised to hear this. "Really?"

"Oh, yes. Christina this and Christina that. He says you are one of the smartest kids in school."

Christina can't help but smile.

"I can see by your smile that you like him, too."

"Sort of."

"Oh, yes, of course. Now back to the shooter. It is in his room. How long will you need it for?"

"Just until Thursday."

"That's fine. When Michael gets home I will tell him where it is in case he looks for it."

She begins to panic. "NO, YOU MUSTN'T TELL HIM."

Mrs. Randolph is confused. "Is there a problem?"

"No, I just... Well, you see, there is... um... um... All right, some of the girls and I are going to surprise the boys by learning to play marbles, but we don't have any. And we want it to be a big surprise."

"Oh, I see. Sort of a way to get their attention?"

"Something like that."

"Well, come then, let's find that shooter so you can get started."

Christina feels a little guilty about telling a white lie, but was it even a lie? After all, they were going to surprise the boys, weren't they?

A few blocks away, Amy is talking to Mrs. Belkin, Jack's mom. She tells a similar "lie" and eventually gets the marble.

Laura approaches Mrs. Saltzman, and Randy's marble is promptly delivered into her hands.

"It will be nice to have that thing out of the house for a while."

Laura smiles. "Thank you, Mrs. Saltzman. I will take very good care of it. And remember, mum's the word."

Michelle is talking to Jeff's mom, Mrs. Samson.

"Well, it is sort of a surprise so we have to be very secretive about it."

Mrs. Samson looks at her and smiles. "Of course you do." And the marble is handed over.

Mrs. O'Brien is more suspicious. "Now tell me again, Sandra, why do you want to surprise Karl?"

Sandra is not good at keeping a straight face and is horrible at dancing around the truth. Once when she was younger she was moved to tears when she confessed to her mom that the tooth fairy left money for her tooth and that she considered keeping the money.

"Oh, Mrs. O'Brien, I... we just want to surprise them."

"You already said that about ten times now, lassie, but I have a strong feelin' there is something brewing in that head of yours that you aren't tellin' Mother O'Brien. Now child, out with it."

Busted, Sandra spills the beans in great detail. After listening to the girl purge her guilt, faster than a federal express commercial, Mrs. O'Brien takes a deep breath.

"Now, child, doesn't it feel better to come clean?"

"Yes, but I feel like I let down the other girls."

"Nonsense, girl. You'll be having Karl's shooter. It is about time you girls stood tall and taught those boys a lesson about the scorn of a woman."

They both start to laugh. Eventually Mrs. O'Brien stops and looks at Sandra, who is laughing so hard there are tears in her eyes. Sandra manages to get out a few words.

"I… can't wait… to… see their faces… when we show them… their own marbles… and…" She takes a deep breath. "By the way, what is the scorn of a woman anyway?"

Sandra starts to laugh again. Mrs. O'Brien can't help herself and starts laughing again, too.

All the girls meet at Christina's house on Wednesday evening. It is a simple house, the walls adorned with awards and commendations presented to her father for heroic deeds performed in the line of his duty as a firefighter. He is the fire chief of the town and well respected. Standing six feet three inches tall, he cuts an intimidating figure, but his friends know him as a gentle giant. His sandy brown hair is cut in a military style, and he has a wide mouth, a chiseled chin, a smile he passed on to Christina, and pale blue eyes the color of a tropical ocean. He and Christina love going to baseball games on the weekend and enjoying hotdogs and soda. By the time they return they are stuffed to the gills. They have a pact never to tell mom how much they ate, yet one look at them and it is obvious what they have been up to.

Her dad tells the girls that the carnival is in town. They all smile because Christina's dad always takes them for a fun-filled evening. Their plan is put on hold until after they return from the carnival. Their favorite game is throwing balls at a target to knock a clown into a giant bucket of water. It never fails to send them into fits of uncontrollable laughter.

Christina's girlfriends watch intently as this massive man picks up a large sledgehammer. His muscles bulge and press against the fabric of his shirt as he swiftly brings down the hammer with all his might. A bull's eye strike sends the metal ball rocketing toward the sky. The bell clangs so loudly that everyone pauses as the echoes ring throughout the carnival grounds. The sound is a signal to everyone that Christina's dad is hammering away.

Following this display of strength, the girls drag him over to the pitching area, where he must remain until each of the girls has a stuffed animal to take home.

Then comes their final challenge. One by one they line up to behold the ride they know will make them all sick. No one wants to be the first to admit she doesn't want to go on it. Those on the ride scream wildly as they are whooshed past. It's a drum-shaped ride in which you stand up while the attendant straps you into your slot. Two padded bars are lowered that firmly hold you in place. After everyone is strapped in, the ride begins turning slowly. Round and round it goes, picking up speed. At first everyone laughs. But as the ride goes faster and faster the laughs turn into screams. Then right when you think it can't get any more intense, the whole thing lifts up and turns at a forty-five-degree angle, spinning so fast that to the people on the ride everything becomes blurred.

The girls exchange glances hoping someone will suggest they do something else, but no one does. Silently they walk to the ticket counter and buy their ticket to sickville. As they reach the window, another girlfriend of Christina's comes running up.

"Hey, guys, have you tried the new ride?"

Eager to jump at any option, Christina replies, "What ride and where is it?"

"It's called the Wild Mouse. It is sort of like a roller coaster, but it whips you around the corners."

All the girls turn with excitement to Christina's dad.

"Can we go on that ride instead of this one?"

He looks at them and cannot miss the pleading expression on their faces.

"Well, it is getting late and you do have school tomorrow. I guess if you don't mind missing this ride... It is up to you all."

Christina goes over to her dad. "We know how much you love this ride, dad, so whatever you want to do it is fine with us."

Christina is good at never letting on that she would rather jump into a tank of hungry piranhas than go on the spinning ride.

"Well, honey, tonight is your night. And since it is a new ride, why don't we try it out. Remember what I have always taught you?"

"Always be willing to try new things."

With that she reaches up to him, and he bends down to receive a hug and a kiss.

They all skip over to the Wild Mouse, silently relieved.

Returning home, the girls head to Christina's room. Her dad sits in his favorite chair, reminiscing about all the years they have been going to the carnival and how grown up his daughter is. He doesn't notice the ringing of the doorbell. Christina's mom looks at her husband and smiles, amused by his daydreaming.

"Don't worry, honey, I'll get that."

Snapping out of it, he says, "What?"

Christina's mom stands just over five feet tall. Though petite, she is kept very fit by her daily five-mile run. A former gymnast, she was offered a place on the Olympic team, but turned it down to get married and have children. She wears a casual but elegant dress. Her shoes are her passion. Each outfit she wears is carefully chosen for its design and price and is perfectly accented by her shoes. Her shoulder-length brown hair is simply styled, with blond highlights. Her perfume is fresh and delicate. She is reminiscent of Grace Kelly with her charm and soft features.

Standing framed in the front doorway, she greets the delivery boy as he walks up carrying the pizza she ordered.

Christina's room is typical for a girl her age, decorated in lacy curtains and collectable dolls. Her vanity table is well organized, with everything carefully positioned. She makes her own bed every morning because she likes it done a certain way. She arranges the extra pillows with the largest in the back, two on each side, and the smallest one sitting proudly in front. The two stuffed chairs beside her bed are covered in soft pink fabric with white bows. The material has a touch of gold thread running through the piping. The skirt hangs to the floor, covering the chairs' stubby legs. When closed, the thick floor-to-ceiling curtains prevent the morning sun from rousing her on Saturday mornings.

Christina's mirror-clad closet doors hide an ample wardrobe of clothing. Interspersed among the details of this feminine environment are athletic trophies, music posters, and martial arts weapons. She excels at martial arts and is rated the best brown belt in her mixed class at the dojo. Her shelves are filled with spy novels and books on covert World War II operations. She is fascinated by undercover stories and fancies herself as an agent while reading them. She loves playing out her fantasies with her girlfriends and is always successful in her missions.

Christina raises the volume on her record player.

"We have to talk softly so no one hears us."

The girls gather together in a conspiratorial huddle.

"Okay, how did you all do?"

One by one the girls take out the shooter each has secured. Amy is the first to present her trophy. It is Jack's marble. Within the clear glass are swirling layers of orange. Each layer is folded back like a piece of paper fanned by the wind and then quickly frozen in time. When it rolls, the clear coat of the outer shell blends with the orange inside, creating a strobe effect. Next it's Laura's turn. She proudly presents Randy's pride and joy. It resembles Jack's marble except the layers inside aren't bent like paper but rather wave evenly throughout the marble. The waves of yellow are thin, almost transparent. Each yellow edge is accented with a rim of dark orange. The more the girls study this marble, the more it looks like a jar of marmalade. As it rolls, the yellow and dark orange visually intermingle, giving it a kaleidoscope effect.

Jeff's marble is ceremoniously unwrapped by Michelle. It is simpler looking than the others. The inside of the marble resembles the head of a Phillip's screwdriver, the only difference being there are only three edges instead of four. Each side fans out like a Venus flytrap, giving it the illusion of six sides. The first side is copper colored, the second side is white with touches of gray toward the center, and the third side is an iridescent blue. Watching this marble roll is like watching a circus clown trying to balance on top of a large ball. Wobbling, a swirling balance of colors, it rolls toward Sandra. She takes out Karl's unusual silver marble. The girls lean forward to have a closer look at the marble's mirror effect. Reflected in the surface is a fisheye view of Christina's entire room and the distorted faces of the girls. Wherever it rolls, the marble takes on the appearance of its environment, always changing and never boring.

Last but not least it is Christina's turn. She reaches into the center of the circle of friends and slowly opens her fist. There, in the palm of her hand, is a perfect cat's eye shooter, a dark center pupil with an almond-shaped blue-green eye. A chorus of ooh and ahs goes up from the girls, signaling the cat's eye's position of royalty, the crème de la crème of the marble world. Christina lowers her hand to the floor, wrapping her finger around the marble, then launches it with her thumb. No matter where you are in the room it appears the eye is watching you. It is a mesmerizing display.

"Good work, girls. Mission accomplished," Christina proudly announces. "They can't say we don't have the best marble since these are all theirs."

The girls cannot stop smiling, and soon it turns into a full-blown giggle-fest as they anticipate the sweet taste of victory.

The cafeteria is typically abuzz with conversation about the upcoming weekend. Michael and his friends sit quietly at their table. They are usually one of the louder tables and draw plenty of attention from the teachers and admiring girls, but not today.

"Okay, guys, I have something to tell you but don't get mad, okay?"

The other boys look at Michael. What could he possibly say that would make them mad at him? Yet each boy is trying to figure out a way to break the news he is silently withholding.

"Well, I went looking for my best shooter and I can't find it." He raises his hand. "Before you say anything, I found another one that is pretty good and I am sure the girls aren't going to have anything nearly as nice as this marble."

No one says a word. They all look down at the floor. Michael feels as though he has let them down.

"Hey, come on, guys, the least you can do is look at it."

Randy looks up at him. "It's not that, Michael. It's just... The same thing happened to me."

One by one the rest of the group fesses up. Michael looks at the others in astonishment as each boy takes out his "backup" marble and shows the others. Despite their odd predicament they all agree their backup marbles will be good enough to beat a bunch of silly girls.

"What are the chances that we all lose our best marble right before the big showdown?"

Michael thinks for a moment. "You guys don't think the girls had anything to do with it, do you?"

Jeff says, "You know, it would make sense, but that would mean Christina and her girlfriends had convinced all our moms to let them have our marbles, and I don't think they have it in them to pull that off."

"I'm not so sure," mumbles Jack. "What do you think, Karl?"

"Come to think of it, my mom was acting sort of weird last night at dinner. She kept asking me what I was going to do at school today, and then she would smile as if she knew something that I didn't."

"I don't know, guys. This all seems too spy novelish," adds Randy.

"Looks like we are about to find out," announces Michael.

"What do you mean?" asks Jack.

"Hi, guys," comes Christina's confident voice. "Ready for our challenge?"

The boys rise out of their seats and proudly exhibit their shooters to the girls. The boys look at one another, their heads bobbing, and force a victory smile.

"Okay, girls, what do you have to show us?" Karl says cockily.

"You never learn, do you?" says Christina, returning his cocky smile. "I must admit that your shooters are excellent and quite beautiful."

"That's pretty big of you to admit," says Jack.

Sandra starts to giggle. "'Pretty big' describes the signs you guys will be wearing tomorrow."

Jeff looks at her as if she is from Venus.

"Well, Sandra, for that to be the case you have to win first."

Laura steps in front of Randy, Amy steps in front of Jack, Michelle positions herself in front of Jeff, Sandra faces off against Karl, and Christina stands in front of Michael. It looks like a scene from West Side Story in which the Jets and the Sharks prepare to rumble. The girls all reach into their pockets and one by one pull out the shooters they have collected, concealing them in closed fists as they wait for Christina to give them the go ahead.

"Ready, girls?" says Christina.

As one they reply, "Ready."

The girls open their hands in unison. The boys gasp as they stare down at their own marbles. Randy, Jack, Karl, and Jeff start complaining that the girls cheated. Michael starts to laugh. The guys look at him.

"What are you laughing at? They stole our marbles."

"Actually, they didn't steal them. They borrowed them from our own mothers, and that I think was very smart. Underhanded but smart."

"Michael, is that an admission of defeat?" asks Amy.

"It would be hard to say we have better marbles than you since those are our best shooters. So, yeah, I would say you beat us."

The girls cheer loudly, and Sandra gives in to hysterical laughter that continues after the other boys and girls have stopped cheering and laughing.

Karl looks at her queerly. "What's up with that laugh?"

"Actually, Karl, it isn't laughter. It's what your mom called scorn of a woman." She starts laughing again and is joined by the rest of the girls as they hand over the shooters, turn around, and strut away.

SIX

Throughout his childhood Joe struggles to come to terms with feelings of loneliness and abandonment. He is drawn to introspective seclusion, and he talks to his mom and dad often--tear-soaked, emotional talks in which he longs for their response. While other boys go off to play at the park, Joe takes walks alone feeling lost. When a friend asks him what he is doing over the weekend, he will fabricate a story about going to a baseball game with his dad. His friends are curious as to why they never see his dad, whom Joe always excuses by saying he is away on important business.

Joe's denial springs from his obsession to ease the pain of his loss. Although he is drawn to sports, he never tries out for any of the school teams. This is because he is afraid the other boys will see that he doesn't know how to play any of the games that he claims he and his dad are playing on weekends. When his grandmother is out of the apartment, he goes into the closest and takes out anything he can find that reminds him of his parents. Joe cries out of loneliness, he cries for the absence of answers, sometimes he cries so hard he vomits. The only thing that ever makes Joe happy is to hear his grandmother talk about his mom and dad.

In high school, Joe's curiosity about his parents becomes a full-blown mission to find out everything he can about them. He begins piecing things together and eventually decides to look into their "accident."

"Grandma, can I ask you something?"

"What is it, Joe?"

"How did mom and dad really die?"

"I'm not sure of your question, Joe."

"Grandma, I am old enough to know the truth."

His grandmother is uncomfortable with his line of questioning.

"I told you, they died in a car accident."

"Grandma, I found some letters in your closet from some of their friends. They talk about the 'murders.' Did you think you could lie to me forever?"

She begins to cry. "I have been trying to spare you the pain of their deaths. Please don't ask this of me."

Joe walks over and puts his arm around her. "Grandma, I have to know the truth. No matter what it is, it has to be better than the stuff in my head. Even if they were criminals--"

"Criminals? Oh no, honey, you've got it all wrong.

"Well then please, Grandma, help me understand."

She takes a deep breath, realizing the time has come for him to know more.

"Your parents were very special. They both worked in intelligence during World War II. While on a mission in Berlin your father discovered documents that pointed to a conspiracy to dominate the world after the war was over. His superiors didn't believe the conspiracy was real, but your dad knew otherwise."

For the next several hours Joe listens carefully to the entire story leading up to the night his parents were assassinated, every detail permanently embedding itself into his mind.

"Where are they buried?"

"I don't know."

"I don't understand."

"All the other families were buried by their immediate family. But when I asked for their bodies I was denied."

"By whom?"

"At the time I thought it was our government."

"And now?"

"Now, I am not sure who it was. They claimed that for reasons of national security the bodies were needed to try to expose the murders. As time went on, I called around trying to find out where they were buried so I could lay flowers on the grave of my son and daughter-in-law—your father and mother. But each time I tried I ran into a wall of bureaucracy. No one seemed to know anything about them. Eventually I gave up."

"Do you know who killed them?"

"I think it was the cartel that they were after."

"Do you know who the cartel members are?"

"No. Your parents knew, and that's what got them killed. I am sorry for never telling you the truth, but at least now you know why."

Joe nodded gratefully. "And now I know what I want to do."

"You sound just like your father."

Joe smiles. "Thanks."

"Joe, these are very dangerous people, and from what I can tell their plot never took hold. You should let it go and try and live some semblance of a happy life."

"I will, Grandma, but I won't rest until the killers are dead."

Throughout high school and into college, Joe dedicates himself to learning everything there is to know about the intelligence world. He has found a purpose in life and will stop at nothing to learn where his parents were buried and who killed them. Driven by obsession, he chooses to apply for MST (Military Science Training) classes, in which he undertakes a deeper understanding of the intelligence community. He decides to enroll in a college that will eventually allow him military access to information. At first his grandmother is opposed to his choice of careers. Eventually she realizes that he is going to do it with or without her support. At the same time she has become convinced the cartel has disbanded. She makes some calls, and over time she is able to help Joe focus on his quest and give him every opportunity to excel and eventually be at the top of his field—just like his father.

Upon graduating from college Joe is actively recruited by every major intelligence agency. He settles on one that offers him a chance to be in the field and work overseas. The agency is part of the War Department/CIA joint effort to train operatives for covert missions. It is a golden opportunity, and he wastes no time in pursuing it. Robbed of a childhood by the death of his parents, Joe finally reconnects with life. He vows never to lose sight of his personal mission. One day at a training seminar Joe is approached by an orderly.

"Excuse me, sir, you have a call."

"Who is it?"

"All I know is that it's a hospital calling for you."

"Grandma…" Joe whispers. He bolts up and goes with the orderly.

"Hello, this is Joe."

"Joe, this is Dr. Richmond. I think you should come to the hospital right away."

Joe hands the phone to the orderly, runs out of the building, and jumps into his car. As he drives to the hospital his eyes fill with tears. He thinks about how much his grandmother means to him and all the ways she helped him get through life without his parents. Soon the sadness turns to anger. In his rage he pulls on the steering wheel so hard he bends it.

When he gets to the hospital he sprints inside, where he is met by the doctor, who tells him his grandmother isn't expected to live through the night. Joe sits in a chair next to her bed, holding her hand and weeping softly. She slowly opens her eyes and turns her head toward him. She squeezes his hand as best she can. She gives him a gentle and reassuring look. Her darling little round-faced grandson has grown into a handsome and confident man. His strong aquiline features are complimented by an engaging smile and dark, welcoming eyes framed by thick black hair.

"Joe, you mustn't cry for me. I have lived a full life, and I want you to do the same."

"Grandma, please don't leave me. You're all I have."

"Sweetheart, it is time for you to have your own life. You are every bit your father and mother. They would have been very proud of the way you turned out."

"Grandma, I love you."

"And I love you. Now, I know why you joined the service, and I want you to promise me something."

"Anything."

"When you find out where they are buried--and I know you will--put some flowers on their grave for me."

"I promise, Grandma."

She smiles at Joe as her hand goes limp. Joe sits there holding her hand and crying, feeling completely alone. All he has left is his personal mission, and he will pour everything into finding a way to accomplish it.

The next day he requests covert operations, an assignment reserved for the very top in the class. With his family gone, the stakes just went up, and whatever is left of the cartel now has a new enemy.

Following special training Joe receives undercover assignments for many years. The work gives him a vast amount of experience and a reputation as a consummate operative. He continues his search for his parents' grave and for signs of the elusive cartel. Joe is handed all the impossible missions. His one hundred percent success rate is unprecedented. As is the case with all operatives who are undercover for extensive periods of time, he is eventually taken out of the field, debriefed, and reassigned. For the time being he will work in the states. Joe is against the change of orders, but he has no choice but to comply. Upon his return, he goes and places flowers on his grandmother's grave. He sits with her for an hour, recalling the joy she brought to his otherwise empty and painful childhood.

The upside to returning is that he now has access to more information than he had while in the field. The high-tech age has come into the mainstream since he first went undercover. Information that was all but inaccessible at the time he entered the field is now but a few keystrokes away. Joe becomes an expert in high tech gadgets and equipment. The government has established a computer network that is the stuff of science-fiction, a web of linked computers with high-level security and brimming with intelligence information. It is a system that is impenetrable... or so they think.

SEVEN

Christina and her friends are saying goodbye and wishing one another good luck at college. Emotions run high because they have been together since they all walked into a schoolroom for the first time. Now for the first time in their lives they will have to make new friends. It is an exciting time for them, but also a scary one. The bond of familiarity will now be challenged.

"Already I can't wait until Christmas so that I can see you all," says Christina.

"Until then let's write each other constantly," adds Sandra.

"Come on, girls, let's not depress each other on our last day together," Laura says with tears in her eyes.

With that they all start to cry, mixing their tears with laughter at themselves for crying. The scene embodies an innocent desire to let go of a childhood that is rich in laughter and memories—formative memories that can never be duplicated. Through the tears they manage to hug, kiss, and say their goodbyes before they drive off in different directions, each of them wondering what lies in store. College will be the last bridge they cross before the real life demands of working, making a living, and starting a family begin to assert themselves.

"All right now, listen up and listen carefully," the water polo coach shouts. "This is a class act we are going up against in both the men and women's divisions. You get caught snoozing and they will ram the ball down your water-soaked throats. We will be away from home so you won't have the home-team advantage. You have to dig deep and find it inside yourselves. Now go shower and get some rest. Tomorrow will be a big day for you all."

The bench empties out as both the men and women head for the locker room.

"Hey, Christina, come here for a minute."

Her heart stops. She knows it can't be about her grades since she is a straight A student. Maybe the coach found out that she went out for a few beers last night with some of her teammates. Coach is a stickler about that, and because she is a junior now a lot more is expected of her. She has no idea what he wants as she walks over to him. One thing she does know is that a good defense is a strong offense. She gives him her best pearly white smile.

"Hey, coach, what a great speech…"

"Cut the crap, Christina. You're not in trouble. Have a seat."

Sitting down, she feels like she is in the principal's office.

"What's up, coach?"

"Listen… As you know, the school doesn't allow me to take the entire team--women or men--when we travel. The bottom line is that I know my women's team will beat theirs. But if we are going to beat the men's team, I need to be able to rely on substitutions. I only have one sub and that's not enough. I need two."

Christina is trying to hold back her excitement at what she hopes will be his next words. It's all she can do to keep from blurting out, *"I'll do it!"*

"The rules allow women to play on the men's team but not the other way around. And since you are the best on the women's team--hell, you're probably better than most of the guys on the men's team--I need you to be a sub. Are you up for it?"

She is about to answer before he goes on.

"Now you realize it will be very rough and the other team will see you as a weak spot. They will come at you with everything. You will have to pull your own weight. I know what I am asking, so if you don't want to do it I won't hold it against you."

She can't take it anymore. "Coach..." He stops talking. "I can handle it. Don't worry, I'll play just as hard as the guys."

"I know. That's what I am afraid of."

"Scared I'll hurt one of them?"

He looks at this strong, beautiful woman that he has coached for the last few years. He knows she will jump at the chance, but he also knows the reality of a woman playing with a bunch of highly strung college males. It is too late for him to worry about it now. The game's afoot and there is no turning back.

The water is extremely turbulent. The noise of the screaming spectators is overwhelming. From beneath the water an object spins clockwise, popping into the air. A hand darts out for the ball, placing the middle finger dead center followed by a rotating arm coming violently forward off the middle finger, causing a backspin to the seven-meter line. The offence and defense both dive for the mishandled ball. Gasps of drawn air echo across the pool as players fill their lungs. A pair of hands grabs the ball and knuckle balls it to his teammate at the three-meter line who instantly shoots and scores.

The score is tied with only one period left. As the ball is put back in play, a brief distraction of the referees gives the other team a chance to elbow the hole set man in the face. He grabs his bleeding nose and jumps out of the water, and the whistle blows.

While the referees and the coaches are arguing, Christina gets ready, knowing she will be called in to substitute. Her heart sends adrenaline coursing through her veins as she realizes the chance to prove herself has finally arrived. Looking into the playing area she sees the opponents sizing her up, and she prepares to enter the water. The other team has transformed into a school of hungry sharks eager for the kill. Whispers of, "Now she will see what it's like to play with the big boys," fuel the testosterone frenzy.

Christina's coach continues to argue for a foul for the overly aggressive move while the other coach claims it was an accident. Christina's coach gives her the signal to get into the water. She turns and sees the bleeding nose of her teammate.

"That must hurt."

"Sure does. And to add to the pain, I'm being replaced by a girl."

"Hey, pal, at least I didn't quit on my team over a little bloody nose. Maybe after the game your mommy can kiss your booboo."

He jumps to his feet ready for a confrontation. Christina reacts and squares off. The other teammates jump in to stop things before they go any further. The coach glances over and sees what is happening. He can't believe his eyes. He runs over to them.

"What do you think you are doing? Isn't it bad enough they are cheating? Now I have to deal with you two playing out high school shit during a match!"

One of the guys turns to the coach. "It wasn't Christina's fault, coach. He antagonized her."

"Okay, wise guy. When we return home, you are suspended for two weeks. You got that? And if I ever hear anyone on this team make any derogatory remarks to anyone, your ass will be off the team. Do I make myself clear?"

They all nod their heads.

"Good. Now let's get back to what we should be doing. Christina, report to the referee and get in the game."

Her blood up, she reports to the referee and gets into the water ready to play her heart out. The other team is poised and ready to end this thing. It is their ball since Christina's team member left the water without permission. The whistle blows and the game resumes. The clock ticks away the minutes as the battle for position and a game-winning point ensues.

Christina takes up the "hole" defense person in front of the goal. As the other team approaches, she lines up in preparation for the driver to pass the ball across the pool to the wing then to her man in front of the goal. She has seen this setup before, and it is often effective.

The hole set man smiles at Christina as he tangles her legs with his, taking her out of position to defend the net. Struggling to keep on top of the water she feels a sharp pain to the center of her back, and then a wild elbow slams into her face, causing a small cut over her eye. Blood drips slowly down her cheek. Her coach is yelling "foul," but once again the referee missed it. The coach looks at her as if to say he is taking her out of the game, but she waves him off. She notices the point man swimming at full speed toward the goal as the hole set man readies to slam the ball into the goal. Christina gets behind him, armed with her own strategy. Closer and closer drives the point man, ready for the pass. He passes to the right wing, trying to throw her off. But she is prepared. She rides her opponent's back, locking her legs around his waist, causing him to go down in the water with her on his back. The wingman gets the ball and passes to what should be his hole set man. Instead, Christina still has her heels hooked into him, and he has sunk down enough for her to reach over him. She rises out of the water and intercepts the ball.

With the momentum now going their way Christina passes the ball to her left wing and signals a play they have rehearsed thoroughly in practice. On her mark, she swims as hard as she can past the point defenseman. The left wing passes the ball to the driver, who is crossing the pool. Picking up his movement, the defense reacts, momentarily ignoring Christina. As the defense closes in on the driver he passes to the point, who finds Christina within one meter of the hole set position. The point man passes to the wing, who instinctively passes to the hole set position. Christina extends her arm completely while kicking with her legs to lift her as far out of the water as possible. All eyes are on Christina. The ball connects with her forward arm motion. The arc of her swing is precise. The curve of the ball is perfectly placed.

As if in slow motion her hand connects powerfully with the ball, back spinning it like a top as it heads for the net. The goalie is anticipating a pass back to the point and is slightly out of position. He reaches for the ball, but his fingertips only brush against it. The spin from her shot is too much for the goalie as it spins into the net. GOAL! The crowd goes wild as the clock winds down.

The buzzer sounds, the whistle blows, and the game is over. The team members converge on Christina. A wild celebration erupts in the stands as the other team looks on, dejected. For the rest of their school years they will have to endure stories about the time they were defeated by a female. Finally the loudspeaker announces that Christina's team has officially won the match. The cheers are deafening. Following the customary handshakes both teams leave the water and head toward the locker rooms.

The bus rolls onto campus and the winning team disembarks. Christina is once again congratulated as she heads to her dorm room. A man approaches her and identifies himself as Special Agent Siwel.

"I see you have a love for the water."

"Yeah, I love playing polo, if that's what you mean. Were you at the game?"

"Are you being solicited by any companies at this time?"

She studies him with some skepticism. "Is this going somewhere?"

"Right to the point, eh?"

"Listen, you identified yourself as special agent..."

"Siwel."

"Right, Siwel. Why don't you tell me what it is you want from me."

"Actually, this is something I would like to offer you."

"And that is?"

"I am, in a sense, a CIA recruiter."

"The CIA? What does this have to do with me?"

"For some time now we have been monitoring your progress in, shall we say, specialized skills. The agency feels that you are a good candidate."

"Which means?"

"Which means we would like to enroll you in various government activities for a short time as part of your training. You would be amongst some of the top agents in the world."

"CIA, special training... Why me?"

"We are embarrassingly thin on female agents with your skill sets."

"And those are?"

"You are a black belt in three different martial art forms, you run six miles a day, you have no police record, and you have never been in trouble. You show leadership qualities as president of your class, you are active in community work, you are a straight 'A' student, you speak three languages fluently, you are highly skilled in the water, you received a prestigious award for your acting, you don't do drugs, and you have achieved the highest ratings in marksmanship in your class. Shall I go on or have you heard enough?"

"Exactly how long have you been spying on me?"

"As I mentioned, I am a recruiter. Much like an athletic recruiter, the CIA pays attention to any young citizen who exhibits natural talents and developed skills."

"You realize I still have to finish college, don't you?"

"We are prepared to wait. Maybe even assist a little."

"I see. What exactly is the pay scale?"

"Lousy, I'm afraid."

"You really know how to recruit, don't you?"

EIGHT

It is a pitch black, moonless night. Stars fill the sky in a breathtaking display. The helicopter cuts through the night just above the water, the calm sea below blending seamlessly with the horizon. Six Navy SEALs await their assignment in silence. The navigator is glued to the GPS. He is tracking the movement of a special class of nuclear sub deep in the ocean. Each SEAL is lost in their private thoughts. Some pray in silence while others close their eyes to catch what might be their last moments of rest for a while. It isn't long before the navigator signals to the pilot he has located the sub and made initial contact.

"Prepare to jump," comes the order. "We are six minutes from the drop point. Our orders are to locate and board the USS Niro."

The SEALs look at one another, knowing it is going to take all of their training to pull off this mission. The USS Niro never surfaces for security reason unless it is in a Navy port for supplies. Surfacing in the open sea means risking identification by the enemy, which can then pinpoint the location. To Naval intelligence this presents the worst-case scenario. This is, after all, the Navy's most highly classified project. Very few people have ever seen this sub, let alone been onboard. It is a self-contained, fully functioning underwater city.

Christina sits quietly amongst her fellow SEALs. She is the first female SEAL to ever earn a position in this elite team. The men welcome and respect her. Now she faces the challenge of her life. Back at base they have gone over the drill ad nauseam until it is ingrained in their minds down to the most miniscule detail. Once the jump is made, a raft will be deployed. Once they have all climbed in, they will send one ping. On this signal the sub will release a blinking buoy that is attached to the sub's hatch door. The team will have one chance at hooking a line to the buoy. The sub will continue at about four knots, never stopping. Once they succeed in hooking onto the line, the raft is towed along the surface while the SEALs prepare for the deep dive, which will last for two and a half minutes.

One by one each SEAL will clip onto the line and begin a descent to the sub below. Once they reach the sub they have fifteen seconds to open a hatch, climb inside, close the hatch, and blow the water out of the hole, giving them life-saving air. Every member of the team will have to execute this maneuver without flaw. Two things are certain: If they miss the hookup they will be lost in the open sea, and if any team member fails to accomplish his or her goal it will jeopardize the entire mission.

"Brandon, you will be the first to go. Christina, you wait thirty seconds and then head out."

The commander then points at the remaining members of the team to assign the order of descent. The helicopter slows to a hover. The time has come. The commander turns to Christina, handing her a packet. This is an honor of the highest caliber. It means she will be the one responsible for delivering the orders to the commander of the sub. Only the President of the United States and Joint Chiefs of Staff know what is inside the package. The male SEALs shake Christina's hand in a show of recognition and support. The helicopter is now hovering like a hummingbird over its designated position. The navigator gives the thumbs up.

The commander looks over his team. "You know the drill. Stand ready."

While hovering ten feet above the churning waves of the cold ocean, one by one the SEALs leave the security of the helicopter for the black water below. The last thing to go out is the raft. Immediately upon hitting the water it inflates. Each team member climbs into the raft and prepares for the mission.

The helicopter disappears into the void of night as Brandon opens the sealed box and sends the signal to the sub. Ping, ping, ping. He waits for fifteen seconds. Ping, ping, ping. After the second set of pings, they all scan in different directions, looking for the blinking light that will signal the hookup target.

After about ten minutes one of the SEALs spots the blinking of the fast-approaching light off the port side. The team goes to work, performing their tasks by the numbers. The drill is now a reality. The hook is fastened to the pole and stands ready. The tie-on to the raft is checked--twice. All eyes are glued to the approaching light, with each team member confirming the distance and rate of speed. The pole and hook is extended over the side of the raft and constantly readjusted.

The blinking light gets closer with each passing second. When it is within one hundred feet of the raft, the hook man leans over the side while two other men hold onto him tightly. The pole and hook are trained on the loop that will pass by momentarily. It is like being on a carousel horse, trying to grab the brass ring. A safety backup man is fastened to the raft loop so if the hook man misses, he will have to secure the loop by hooking his arm through it. He is fully aware that by doing this he risks being pulled into the water and drowned. It is the most dangerous job on the mission, and as such it is assigned on a strictly voluntary basis. If he is needed tonight he will have four seconds once he is in the water to attach the raft loop to the blinking buoy. Being hooked to the raft will be the last attempt at ensuring the success of the mission.

Each second begins to stretch out as the anticipation builds. It is so quiet that each heartbeat becomes a deafening drone. Their lives are at stake, and they know it. The buoy is now fifty feet and closing. Forty... thirty... twenty... ten... The pole and hook are in position. The backup man is readied.

The blinking buoy comes alongside the raft as the hook man pushes the loop out, snagging the blinking buoy perfectly. The second man quickly sets another cable loop to the raft. With a strong tug, the raft, now connected to the hatch of the sub below, is dragged across the ocean surface. The backup man lets out a sigh of relief. They all smile reassuringly.

Using the cable as a guide, each member has to swim down to the sub, open the hatch, climb inside, close the hatch, seal the air lock, blow the water, pressurize, climb inside the sub, and refill the lock with water in preparation for the next member. The journey down to the sub is the hardest part. It is a descent into darkness for almost two and a half minutes against the current of a moving sub with no air tank. Losing your hold on the cable for any reason means being lost at sea--a sure death sentence.

The team readies itself. Special gloves with raised rubber dots give the SEALs added traction on the cable. Brandon regards the other members with a strained look on his face. Christina knows that something isn't right.

"Brandon, we have been trained for this, you can do it."

He looks at her without saying a word. She pats him on the shoulder. "It's time."

With that, Brandon begins a series of deep inhalations to expand his lungs to their limit before filling them with as much air as possible. While he does this, two other members help Christina secure the package to her back. She needs her hands free to pull herself down as rapidly as possible to the submarine's hatch. Brandon leans over the side and hooks himself to the cable. With a final inhalation he disappears into the water. A temporary tug on the raft signals his body weight is fighting the pull of the sub, the current of the sea, and his struggle to pull himself down to the hatch.

The last team member clicks on the stopwatch to begin the count. At thirty-second intervals another team member goes into the water. Fifteen seconds pass, and Christina prepares to go in. At five seconds left she hooks herself to the cable.

"Now," cries the timer.

Without hesitation Christina slips into the sea. The tug comes and she disappears. The water is freezing cold against her face as she pulls herself hand over hand toward the life-giving hatch below. She counts the seconds to help her focus on the descent. Twenty seconds passes and her confidence rises. She feels stronger with each pull of her hands . . .

Then without warning something slams into her face. She is pushed back toward the surface twice as fast as she was going down. It knocks some of the air out of her lungs. She loses her grip on the cable, but the loop is still attached. She spins around and around the cable like a ball tied to a string on a pole. She is in a fight for her life, still with no idea of what has slammed into her.

As she continues her ascent, she grabs for the cable to stabilize herself. As she reaches out, a pair of hands grabs her. She begins to struggle, thinking it is an assault. The struggle continues as both bodies cling to the cable, slamming into each other while spinning out of control, neither gaining any advantage over the other. The air in her lungs is heating up. She senses the desperation of her situation and hopes she will reach the surface before anything else can happen. She reaches down to her boot and begins unstrapping her knife. If this is to be a fight to the death, then she wants to win it.

The bodies collide once again. Now Christina finds herself wrapped in the arms of the other person, unable to unsheathe her knife. The pressure of the hold increases, and the air is squeezed out of her lungs.

Onboard the raft, the timer is counting down from fifteen. When he reaches eight seconds two bodies breach the water. Both are gasping for air. Christina slams her forehead into the face of the other person, who goes limp. The team members pull the two bodies into the raft. It is Christina and Brandon. After catching their breath, she grabs Brandon, who is now coming to, and begins shaking him.

"You stupid son-of-a-bitch, you could have killed us both. What the hell are you thinking?"

He looks up at the team. "I'm sorry, I lost it. I can't do this."

They look at one another knowing they can't leave him on the raft alone. They have to get him to the sub, but how? Desperate glances pass among them as they hope for an idea or some viable solution. Time is wasting away, and their mission is becoming critically jeopardized.

"I have an idea," says Christina. "When I get to the sub, I will hook an auxiliary line to the hatch and send it back up on a float. Attach it to Brandon–he'll be last to go down. Brandon, I will tug it three times and then begin pulling you down to us."

Brandon buries his head.

"Brandon, look at me." He regards her with a look of embarrassment. "You need to focus. We all go through these moments. Don't forget we are a team. We are not going to leave you here. When we start to pull, you have to help by climbing down the cable as fast as possible. No matter what happens, do not give up on us. You understand?"

Sheepishly he nods his head. With that, each team member places his hand on Brandon's shoulder for support. Christina looks up to the sky and closes her eyes. She begins her preparation again. This time, she is the first to go down. Before she goes in, she turns to the timer.

"Hold sending anyone until you see the buoy with the new cable for Brandon. I will have to explain this to the commander and rig something up."

With that she takes one last breath and slips into the water for the second time.

NINE

True to lore, New York City never sleeps. Teeming with every walk of life, it is a place where anyone can remain anonymous or, if they choose to, disappear forever. It came of age with the Industrial Revolution and is a global nexus of art and culture.

The prestigious Waldorf Astoria Hotel is a world-famous landmark with a rich history. There patrons are treated like royalty and guaranteed absolute privacy. It is a place where the super-rich conduct secret business and lovers' rendezvous are discreetly consummated. It is a place of solitude, a relative oasis embedded amidst the busy hustle and bustle of city streets thronging with condensed crowds moving at top speed to appointments and commitments in a mad scramble for the almighty dollar. Bluntness bordering on rudeness is a way of life in this culture and never taken as a serious offense by those living in the city. Street vendors peddle their wares to Wall Street tycoons. Children look for any opportunity to cash in on someone, be it stranger or friend. Skyscrapers jut high into the sky, casting foreboding shadows over what would otherwise be sunny streets. People make mad dashes across busy streets, knowing full well the cars approaching aren't going to stop for them. Some try to forget the fact they live in one of the largest cities in the world by escaping to Central Park for a walk, but they always keep a watchful eye out for would be muggers. Nothing is sacred or safe, but after all, this is the city where, if you can't find it here, then it probably doesn't exist.

On the top floor in a suite, its shades drawn shut, an unidentified group sits around a table covered with black-and-white photos of men and women. The lights are low and faces barely visible through the cigarette and cigar smoke.

"We need one more member to complete our task group.

"Who is the top choice?" says a voice brimming with authority.

A hand reaches out and spreads the photos in a line. The hand sports a diamond ring with the symbol of the Freemasons on its side. A Rolex wraps around the sun-tanned wrist.

A woman's finger points to one of the photos.

"This one. His background is clean. No parents, no wife, and he is black-OP trained. He is our best man and has an impeccable success rate."

"Any children?"

"No, sir."

"We also have the perfect operative to recruit him."

"Good work. What's his name?"

Two naked bodies fall onto a bed.

"Oh, Joe," she moans softly.

The cool summer breeze blows the curtains gently, juxtaposing the aggressive passion taking place on the bed. Christina stretches languorously, her lean, curvaceous body like a work of art. She moves Joe's hands to her breasts, and he fondles them with just the right amount of pressure to send Christina's head back in ecstasy. The rhythm of her body incites his passion. His lips meet hers in a succulent ballet. Moving down her neck, he cups her breast with his hands as his tongue moves the hardened nipple into his mouth. His lips clamp down gently on her excited nipples. With her nipple fully engulfed in his warm, wet mouth, Christina massages the back of Joe's head, pulling on his hair with each tug of his mouth.

After several minutes, Joe takes Christina's breasts in his hands. Placing his face between them, he takes a deep breath, inhaling the scent of her skin mixed with the delicate perfume she wears. He plants a trail of wet kisses between her breasts, moving downward toward her stomach, where the muscles begin to quiver. As he passes her navel, her legs begin to shake in anticipation of his mouth on her now open and waiting womanhood. The sounds of her joyous climax find the open window and echo among the residential high-rises of midtown.

Pulling him toward her, she rolls him onto his back and kisses him hard. Joe is every bit as fit as Christina, his strong, muscular body like that of a Greek athlete. Sitting upright on top of him, she begins to rub his chest. As her hands move over his body, she moves in a womanly rhythm that is the stuff of male fantasy. Her long blonde hair sweeps over his chest and stomach, exciting him to the point of pain. Christina takes him into her mouth. Lost in pleasure, Joe takes deep, irregular breaths. It feels as if a silk scarf has been wrapped around him and is being pulled tighter and tighter. With each bob of her head his body arches in delight. Pausing for a second, Christina looks up at Joe with adoring eyes.

"I want you," she whispers.

She slides her long fingers up his body, wrapping his face in her hands. The movement of their bodies becomes involuntary as they couple intensely. The cool breeze of the night is no match for the heat of their bodies. They move faster and faster, exchanging deep, passionate kisses. Perspiration beads and then drips from their pulsating bodies. Their mutual pleasure attains its full measure in a fiery explosion that leaves in its wake a stillness in the air. Fully spent, they fall side by side on soft down pillows, breathing heavily. The ceiling fan does little to quench their utter exhaustion.

After a few moments, Joe gets up and leaves, returning with two glasses and a bottle of champagne as Christina props herself up against the headboard. They clink glasses. Joe lies next to her, and she snuggles into his arms.

"It's hard to believe we've only known each other for three months."

He gives her a warm a smile. "You make me feel really... special."

"Careful there, Mr. Confirmed Bachelor," she teases.

Setting her champagne glass on the end table, she notices a war medal. She picks it up to examine it closer.

"Was this your father's?"

"Yes, it was."

They are silent for a while. She puts down the medal and sits facing him.

"Joe, do you ever wonder what it would have been like to know your parents?"

"Only every day. I have access to the best technology on the planet, and I still can't find out much about them."

She is pensive for a moment.

"What if--I mean, just pretend for a moment-- there was a way?"

Joe smiles. He kisses her on the cheek. "Nice thought. It would be a childhood dream come true."

She gets out of bed and puts on a bathrobe. Her tone turns serious as she walks away from him.

"Joe, we have to talk."

He is slightly concerned. "Problem in Blissville?"

She looks him in the eye. "Not exactly." She takes a moment and begins. "During World War II your father and a small group of commandos infiltrated Nazi headquarters. While he was on operation 'Paper Cut' he came across documents that pointed to a global conspiracy involving a select group of Nazi officials and American Industrialists."

After a brief silence Joe laughs. "God, Christina, you almost had me. I didn't know you were a writer."

"I'm not kidding."

Joe gets out of bed, puts on his bathrobe, and goes over to her.

"If you're not joking, Christina, then how did you come across this information and why are you telling me?"

With searching eyes, she says, "Because I know how much it means to you. And…" Looking at Joe, she thinks to herself, this wasn't supposed to happen. Joe senses something doesn't fit

"This is sounding worse by the minute, Christina. Why don't you take a deep breath, relax, and then tell me what's going on here?"

She brushes his hand with her fingertips. "Promise you won't hate me?"

Joe doesn't respond.

"Oh, shit, you're not making this easy."

"Easy? You're talking about parents I never knew as if you know them." He begins to grow angry. "Talk to me, Christina. What do you know about my parents and how do you know it?"

She studies his face and wonders how things ever got so crazy. If she tells him, she may lose him. If she doesn't tell him, the mission will be in jeopardy. She feels torn between her emotions and her sense of duty. Finally, she begins.

"I belong to a group of American operatives formed to dismantle a cartel, whose plans were discovered by your father on a mission called 'Paper Cut'. They are the same people who killed your parents."

Joe has a sinking feeling in his stomach. "Are you telling me that you're an Op? And if you are, then all this has been part of some recruiting assignment?"

Christina tries to hug him. He pushes her away and quickly gets dressed.

She hangs her head and continues. "Yes... I was sent to recruit you into our group. Your profile is perfect."

"My profile for what? Being used for sex and hurting my feelings? You're good, Christina. I need to take a walk... get some fresh air."

Joe opens the door and begins to leave.

"The files are in the computer," she blurts out.

He pauses at the door without turning around. She continues.

"The file can be located in the War Department's WW II operations classified TOP SECRET PC427. It will also tell you where your parents are really buried."

Joe doesn't know what to think. He stands framed in the doorway feeling betrayed and abandoned once again. He was beginning to think that love had finally found him and his life could begin recuperating from some of the damage it had suffered over the years.

"When you are finished getting dressed, Christina, just go."

Joe sighs and leaves, closing the door behind him. Christina sits quietly in a chair. After a while she picks up the phone and dials. She watches the closed door in Joe's apartment and eventually says softly into the phone, "The bird is being trained."

Joe sits searching the database of a CIA computer when he comes across a file labeled: War Department - Top Secret PC427 - Classified. Every time he tries to access the file the same message comes up: Access Denied. Eventually he grows frustrated. He stares out the window thinking about how close he is to finding another piece of the puzzle to his parents and his shattered past.

A breeze disturbs some of the papers on his desk. The smell of summer starts him thinking about all the time he has spent with Christina. He thinks about the passionate nights, the long walks, and the intimate conversations during sleepless nights. It is an openness he has never experienced with any other woman. And it all seems to be slipping away into the shadows of yesterday. He is certain they had connected on many levels.

How could his perceptions have been so far off? Where were those red flags that should have signaled him? Was he slipping as an agent? Was he so easily fooled by the lure of sex or the pretense of love? Had he become so consumed by his pain that he confused passion with love? A battle rages in his head to the point he wants to scream. Could he have been that blind about her or did she really have feelings for him? He knows what the training is like and the level of focus required if they expect to succeed. But something inside him wants to believe this is different. He doesn't want this to be his typical MO. Love them and leave them before any type of commitment sets in.

Joe gets up and stretches, shaking off these unwanted thoughts. He clears his head, and immediately an idea presents itself. He picks up the phone and dials a number. His friend Jimmy works for the War Department in operations and research. The room is a beehive of activity, with people busying themselves at various stations. This room is research headquarters for any and all War Department operative information. Jimmy keeps a sign over his desk:

If You
Can't Find
A File,
It's Because We Are
Hiding It.

"Jimmy, this is Joe. I need a favor."

"Name it."

"I want access to a file." Joe is very anxious and sounds it.

Jimmy continues to perform his duties as he speaks to Joe. Nothing fazes Jimmy; he has seen it all.

"Which one?"

"Paper Cut. PC427."

"Okay, let's have a look." Jimmy punches buttons on his keyboard and brings up the file. Beneath the file is an access code.

"Got it." Jimmy looks again at the screen. "Wow. What do you want with this puppy?"

"It's personal." Joe will not stop until he has the file.

"This one's too hot."

Joe cannot believe those words just came out of Jimmy's mouth. He bolts out of his chair and screams into the phone.

"Too hot?" Joe squeezes the phone receiver so tightly that his knuckles turn white. "Let's talk about how hot it was on Operation Toothpick? You remember when they almost had you..."

Jimmy knows what Joe is about to say and doesn't want to be reminded.

"Okay, jeez... You don't forget, do you?"

"Glad to see you don't either. What's the code?"

In a carefully executed move, Jimmy scans the room to see if anyone is eavesdropping. He whispers his reply into the receiver.

"OP-WWII-SPLS-XDCBF01010119-PC427. One last thing you should know. They were buried under assumed names so that no one, including you, could ever locate them. The name was Poisson. Now we are even. I gotta go."

Before Jimmy hangs up the phone, Joe is already accessing the file. He begins reading. His imagination stimulated by this turn of events, Joe's mind wanders, directed by his emotions.

The details of a photograph materialize slowly in photographic solution. The photograph shows what appears to be a document. Tongs reach into the bath and ripple the solution. Joe's father removes the photos and hangs them up to dry. He starts to read the document and his eyes widen, his expression one of conviction. He dries his hands, turns on the light, and dials a number.

"Hello?"

"Hi, baby. Remember the secret room I found on Operation 'Paper Cut'?"

Sure, why?"

"Well, I am staring at the developed pictures."

"Is it what you suspected?"

"Worse. I'm going to take this to the top."

"Before you do, at least make a duplicate."

"Good idea."

"We can hide it in the usual place."

Joe shakes his head clear and returns to reality. He reads the last line on the screen with tearful awe:

As a result, operative Gus and his wife were terminated due to suspicion of wartime espionage and considered a National Security Threat. Their three-year-old son was given to his grandmother.

....End Report.

Joe sits back, lost in his thoughts. He shuts off the computer, gets his coat, and slowly walks out of his office.

The clock reads 2:30 AM. Christina is on her balcony smoking a cigarette. Under the light of the full moon, her body aches for Joe's touch. The city is quiet and still, with the building lights burning throughout the sleepless night. On the street below a man walks his dog. Steam swirls into the open air from manhole covers. A street sweeper trudges along, doing his small part to clean up the concrete jungle.

BANG, BANG, BANG, comes a loud knock on the door, upsetting the solitude and startling Christina. Flicking her smoke into the street below, she reaches for her gun and goes to the door.

"Who is it?" she asks with gun poised.

"It's Joe."

She sets the gun on the table and begins to unlock the series of deadbolts that most New Yorkers take for granted. She opens the door and smiles, happy to see him. Instantly she realizes he is pissed. Without a word, Joe grabs her by the shoulders and slams her against the wall.

"Okay, Christina, just what the hell kind of game are you playing here?"

"It's not a game. I can only tell you what I know." She struggles to free herself without success.

"I want the truth, Christina." He is now nose-to-nose with her. "The truth."

Christina looks into his eyes. She knows behind his mask of anger is a gentle, loving man who wants to belong to someone. She understands the passion that motivates his quest for knowledge.

"Isn't that all any of us want?" she asks gently.

Joe relaxes his grip. He turns away from her, embarrassed by his loss of control. Before meeting Christina, he had almost convinced himself that he would never know the truth about his family. Then she had reopened deep wounds—wounds that had already bled his heart dry. Suffocating from overwhelming emotions once buried, he collapses on her couch. She goes and sits beside him quietly for several moments.

"It all started with what your father discovered on his mission inside Nazi Germany. Since then, group after group of black ops have tried to infiltrate the cartel to disrupt their plans."

"What plans?"

"Joe, I know this is the last thing you want to hear, but unless you are in the group, I can't disclose that to you. As an agent I'm sure you appreciate the need for secrecy. However, I do have something that will tell you where your parents are buried."

She walks over and opens the closet. She reaches inside searching for something. Suddenly she stops. She turns around to find Joe has his gun trained on her.

"Nice and slow, Christina."

"You going to shoot me for having sex with you?"

She slowly withdraws her hand from the closet, pulling out an envelope. She tosses it on the couch. He looks at the envelope and then at the gun in his hand. Lowering the gun, Joe reaches for the envelope.

He stares down at it in his hands, his indecision on whether or not to open it evident in his bearing.

Christina sees writ in Joe's expression the dilemma he faces, of whether to risk potentially opening a Pandora's Box or simply leave the envelope sealed and his past and its painful memories without resolution. Despite being emotionally drained Christina makes another attempt to reach him.

"Joe, you have to believe what I have told you."

"I really don't know what to believe, Christina."

Joe holsters his gun, slips the envelope in his pocket, and leaves.

The next day is picture perfect. The deep blue sky is populated with billowing clouds that shift and morph, resembling one second an animal, the next a face, and the next something drawn from a fantastic dream. The hot sun makes it the perfect day to lie on the beach. Horseshoe crabs line the sandy shore with their prehistoric saw-like blades scaring the kids, who scream and run to the safety of their parents.

The sunbaked beach is like a hot skillet, compelling those daring or foolish enough to go barefoot to make mad dashes across the blistering sand. Everyone heads toward the cold seawater as the air fills with a chorus of, "Ouch, ooh, ouch..." Occasionally each firewalker glances up briefly to see how much farther it is to the soothing waters of the Atlantic Ocean. Sweat drips down their faces, not only because of the heat but because their scramble to the sea entails the only exercise they've had in a year. Many look up only to realize they are just halfway there. Torn between retreating or pushing on, a few warriors let out a cry of, "Geronimo!" With arms flailing and hopping from foot to foot, they begin to resemble a spastic cartoon character falling off a cliff.

The waves break, bathing their red-hot feet in cool, foamy water as others follow suit into the revitalizing shallows of the ocean. Temporarily relieved, they look up to see a wave about to crash on top of them, sending bodies swirling to the ocean bottom and filling swimsuits with sand. Thump, thump, thump go bodies until heads spring up into the air, spitting out saltwater and gasping for air before laughing at the thrill of it all.

This is high time at the Jersey shore. It is on such days that Joe especially misses not having known his mother and father. In place of memories of them having shared days such as this, today Joe stands under those same clouds and that same hot summer sun, waiting to complete a lifelong journey to visit his parents' gravestones.

Joe feels awkward, not knowing what to say. He is overwhelmed by the thought of finally reaching his childhood dream. There before him is the long overdue physical evidence of what he lost as a child. His eyes are moist and his body stiff. He takes a few slow breaths and takes in the unkempt gravesite.

"I'm sorry we never had a chance to be together. It would have been nice... I mean different... I mean... Anyway, Grandma was very good to me and always gave me what I needed. Speaking of Grandma, I promised her something..."

Joe places the flowers gingerly on the grave and seems once again at a loss for words, then a smile spreads across his face.

"She wasn't thrilled with the idea of me going into the service, but she supported me through the hard times. I wish we could have been together like a normal family."

Joe is again distracted by thoughts of what could have been. Tears fill his eyes. Finally, he falls to his knees.

"Mom and Dad, if you can hear me, I hope you are proud of how I turned out."

He reaches down and touches the earth where his parents have been laid to rest.

From across the cemetery a camera with a telephoto lens takes a picture of Joe kneeling and talking. CLICK. Another picture is snapped as Joe lifts up his head and fills the camera's frame.

Joe pulls himself together, and his thoughts turn to revenge. His hands clutch at the earth.

"Whatever it takes, I will find out who did this to us, and if they are still alive, I'm going to make sure they wish they weren't."

He stands, dropping the dirt back onto the grave through clenched fists. He takes one last look before saying goodbye to the parents he never got a chance to know. He turns and begins to walk away. Suddenly he stops, his head tilted, and turns back to the grave. He walks back and looks at the headstone. It reads:

Here Rests Gus, A Dedicated Patriot.

Joe reads it several more times. Something doesn't sit well. Looking at the headstone, he realizes what is wrong.

The footsteps that echo in the massive entranceway seem out of place for the library. For a place that is supposed to offer solace and quietude, it is causing nothing but stress for Joe. He scans yet another microfiche, desperately hoping to find his parents' obituary. It is a bittersweet moment; one he has dreamed about time after time without any apparent hope of fulfillment. Today he had found his first real clue, and he isn't about to give up until he finds what he came looking for: the truth.

Joe rubs his eyes. He has been reading for several hours without a break. As he examines the last of the listings he finds his father's obituary. He thinks, could this really be the end of my search? He knows that reading on means there will be no turning back. He will have the long-awaited answers to his questions. Yet knowing this scares the hell out of him. Because having this new information will ultimately lead to a whole new set of questions.

He stretches his back and bends from side to side, thinking about Christina. What if she knows more than she is letting on? What if she is sending me on some sort of wild goose chase? Is there any way I can trust her? After all, she did "recruit" me by using sex.

Joe is still feeling betrayed, angry, and once again abandoned. His emotional stability has been undermined, leaving him a shell of his former self. It appears there is nothing left for him but to go forward and play out the hand he has been dealt. No matter what he reads it will change all he knows and all he believes to be reality.

Taking a deep breath, he reads the obituary. A chill runs through his body. He reads it two more times then shuts off the machine and quickly leaves the library.

Nestled amongst tall maple trees is a hundred-year-old stone bridge with an adolescent stream running beneath its archway. The bridge has seen more than its share of history. It is a bridge to inspire patriotic speeches issued to troops about to go into battle, a bridge for politicians to stand on and give environmental speeches, a bridge for boys and girls to play around while letting their imaginations run wild.

The bridge embodied a host of stories while collecting new ones from the generations of people who crossed over or passed underneath its archway. This is where Joe and Christina agreed to meet. Walking together in silence over the bridge is an awkward moment for the both of them. Another story is about to be handed down to the stony gatekeeper of history.

Joe looks at her. "Thanks for meeting me."

"I wasn't sure if you ever wanted to see me again."

Taking a long deep breath, he says, "I went to my father's grave last week."

They continue walking in silence. A bicyclist races past them. Rollerbladers push themselves to their limits, drawing exhausted breaths. A young boy buys a hot dog from a street vendor as his sister munches on cotton candy. The water running beneath the bridge beckons for young and old alike to partake in a round of splashing in the relentless summer heat.

Although Joe and Christina stroll side by side they are miles apart, neither of them knowing what to say. Joe stops walking and looks her in the eye.

"Is there something else you want to tell me?"

Stopping to face him, she says, "What else do you want to know?"

He is agitated. "Do you think this is a game or is this still an assignment to you?"

"I guess I deserved that."

"If you know something that can help settle my past for me, then tell me."

"What can I tell you that would help?"

Joe looks at her with penetrating eyes. "How about what happened to my mother?"

Christina looks like she is going to vomit. Joe notices and pushes harder.

"I was standing at their graves when I realized the headstone said nothing about my mother."

Christina is in turmoil over whether or not to tell Joe the rest of what she knows. Then something occurs to her and she sees a perfect opportunity to complete her assignment and help Joe at the same time.

"If I tell you, will you join the group?"

Joe turns and takes in the view from the bridge. Christina goes over to him.

"All right, Joe, I owe you this. But remember, I'm just the messenger."

Joe continues looking away from her. All he wants are answers to his burning questions. He will stop at nothing until he gets them. Christina finally works up the courage and tells him what he already suspects. "Your mother is still alive."

TEN

Joe drives through a middle-class neighborhood scanning the addresses. The New Jersey suburbs are like a different country compared to the hustle and bustle of the city. The streets are lined with immense weeping willows and other long-established flora. The lawns are immaculate and teeming with laughing children hard at play.

Joe wonders if this is the type of life he missed out on. Would he have been one of these happy children? He looks over the street names and finally sees Valley Road. He turns the corner and sees the house with the number he is looking for. A lump forms in his throat. Will she recognize him? What will she say? Who is this woman? But the most important question he has long wondered comes screaming to his mind: WHY DID SHE ABANDON ME? Why didn't she want him?

His thoughts get away from him. If my husband had just been assassinated, then why wouldn't I want my only child? He shakes his head to clear it. Joe stares at the house, gripped by paralyzing fear.

His thoughts begin to tense like a vise grip tightening in his mind. Do I have the strength to deal with this? He knows there is no turning back. His life to this point has just ended. There is only that which lies ahead. A future filled with more uncertainty from a mother who abandoned him and a supposed girlfriend who has betrayed his trust. It is an ugly way to begin a new life.

Getting out of his car, he approaches the front door. With each step the path seems to grow longer and longer. The sun beats down on him, drying his mouth and forming sweat beads on his forehead. He sympathizes with what it must feel like to suffer from thirst, desperate for a lifesaving sip of water in the middle of the desert.

He imagines himself as a small child coming home from school and having his mommy greet him at the door with chocolate milk and cookies. Mustering a child-like sense of courage, he reaches across his lost years of childhood for the doorbell and hesitantly pushes it. The button feels huge against his child-size finger. The worn-out white button sinks into its casing with a BUZZ, bringing Joe back to his senses.

After a short time, the door opens, bringing to an end his lifelong journey of pain and insecurity. An elderly woman stands before him. She is dressed in impeccable clothing. Her well-kept hair is mostly white and accented by an antique hairpin matching the one on her lapel. Her shoes are clean and polished. Her dress is an imitation Dior and perfectly appropriate for summer. She wears a tasteful amount of jewelry and no wedding ring.

Joe stares at this stranger with his heart racing. So often he has fantasized about what he would say and how it would be if this moment ever came to pass. His mouth opens several times but nothing comes out. He has no idea how to begin. The woman smiles warmly at Joe.

"Yes, dear, may I help you?"

Coming out of his trance, he stammers, "I don't know where to start. I guess the best way is to just come out and say it."

She looks at him with genuine concern. "Is there something wrong, young man?"

"No… I think… well, it's just that… I think you might be my mother."

The woman's expression changes from one of kindness to a look of confusion and terror. "You must be mistaken. I never had children."

"I imagine this must be difficult for you. Could we just…. maybe we could… I have so many questions to ask."

"I told you, I never had any children. Now go away before I call the police."

She slams the door and locks it. Joe stands there numb, frustrated, and finally he blurts out the only thing he can think of.

"I know about the operation in Germany." Joe continues searching for words to say. "Please listen to me. I AM YOUR SON," he screams. "I know about what happened to Dad."

From the other side of the locked door, she says,

"I don't know what you are talking about. Now please go away."

"I read the file."

Joe is about to explode. He is so close. But how will he ever know the truth unless she talks to him? All the years of frustration, loneliness, and endless tear-filled nights come barreling out of his mouth.

"FOR CHRIST'S SAKE, HE WAS ASSASSINATED FOR WHAT HE BELIEVED IN." He leans his head against the door and softly whispers, "Please don't let them win."

After a moment Joe hears the woman crying. He tries to control himself. He puts his hand on the door as if to comfort his crying mother.

"I know this must be upsetting after all these years. But please… I have spent my entire life not knowing what happened to you and Dad. Why won't you talk to me?"

She continues to cry, speaking through her sobs. "You don't understand. I can't see or talk to you."

"Give me one good reason."

She doesn't answer. It feels hopeless. Joe lifts his head from the door.

"I remember one night when I was young. We were in our living room in the apartment. Dad put you behind a blanket saying he could make you vanish. He said, all right, Joe, watch this. He held the blanket up with you behind it as he said the magic words. When he lowered the blanket, you were gone. I was shocked. I asked him, "Where did Mom go, Dad?" He looked down at me and said, Joe, it is magic.

"I got up and started looking behind every door and in every room. Dad tried throwing me off track by telling me you weren't in the apartment at all. Finally, I got to the bathroom door and was about to go in to see if you were hiding there. In my heart I somehow knew you were behind that door holding back a laugh, but I didn't let on. Finally he said, Come on, Joe, why would your Mom hide in a bathroom?" Joe smiles at the memory, one of the only ones of his Dad. "I know who you are. Please talk to me. I need to know why you never tried to find me."

Joe stares at the door with a sinking feeling that it will remain shut forever. He will never know his mother. Resigned, he turns and begins walking back to his car. Halfway up the path he hears the door being unlocked. He turns around, and standing there in the doorway is Pauline, crying and smiling and with arms outstretched.

"I am so sorry, honey."

Joe walks to his mother and embraces her, the pain of a lifetime distilled into a few precious seconds of forgiveness.

"Why? I don't understand. I always thought you both were dead." It takes a minute for her to muster the courage to speak of things she had buried deep in her mind long ago.

"After they shot us, I tried to save your father, but he was dead within minutes. I tried so hard. I watched the life leave his eyes. It was horrible. I felt so helpless." She begins to sob.

"But what happened later? Why didn't you come for me?"

Joe's eyes are watery.

"Oh, Joe, I wanted to. I wanted to more than life itself. You were my baby and the only piece of your father I had left." She pulls herself together. "While I was recuperating in the hospital, I was visited by a member of the cartel. He told me that they would let me live with the proviso that I was never to contact you for any reason for the rest of my life. It was their way of sentencing your father and me."

"That's what stopped you? I don't get it."

"Joe, watching your father die in my arms was hard enough," she says, trying to control her emotions. "The man told me if I ever saw you or talked to you they would torture and kill you before my eyes. Then they would kill me." She loses it in his arms as she holds onto him for dear life. "Can't you see? I HAD NO CHOICE. I couldn't let that happen. Oh God, please forgive me. I have missed you so much."

Overwhelmed, Joe awkwardly hugs her back. They hold each other. After a few minutes and without a word, she leads him into the house. The front door closes and Joe's life begins again.

Lying on top of the coffee table in Pauline's sitting room are a few photos along with a locket. She picks up the locket, opens it, smiles, and hands it to Joe.

"This is one of the only surviving pictures of you and your Dad together."

Joe looks at the picture. He is filled with emotion.

"What do you mean one of the only ones that survived?"

"After your father died, there was a fire in the place we were living. I ran back in to try and save as much as I could. The locket, some pictures, and this cross are all I managed to grab before the firemen dragged me out. I want you to have these."

Joe puts the cross around his neck and tucks it under his shirt. He puts the photos and the locket in his pocket. Little does he know that in so doing he has taken possession of the keys to the hiding place that holds all the documents. He now has the knowledge and elements to bring down the cartel and end their plan. It all hinges on him discovering the locket's secret.

Joe struggles with whether he should ask his burning question or if he should wait awhile. Deciding he has already waited a lifetime; a calm comes over Joe as he looks at his mother.

"Do you know who murdered Dad, and does anyone else know what he knew?"

She pulls out a monogrammed handkerchief and wipes her eyes. "Joe, this is all a bit much. I think we should take it slow and easy for a while."

Joe sees how upset this is making his mother and nods his head in agreement.

The following day, Joe feels profoundly renewed and looks forward to embarking on his new life. He is filled with hope thinking about his conversation with his mother. Yet his unresolved issues surrounding his father's assassination continue to creep into his mind. The endless haunting questions gnaw at his euphoria until it is replaced with anger destined to be unleashed on the world unless he directs it properly. After his ritual walk to the bitter coffeepot, Joe returns to his desk, picks up the phone, and dials.

The instant someone picks up on the other end of the line Joe blurts out, "Christina, please."

A brief moment later she arrives. "Hello, this is Special Agent Christina. May I help you?"

Joe sits there holding the phone for a few seconds. In that short time he flashes back over his entire life leading up to meeting his mother. He now knows how to direct his explosive anger.

Christina repeats, "Hello, this is Special Agent Christina. May I help you?"

His reply is simple. "I'm in."

Christina's eyes widen. She has now completed her assignment. So why doesn't it feel right? She begins to scribble on a piece of paper, trying to distract herself from the unpleasant mixture of emotions and accomplishment that she is experiencing. She is completely unaware of how pent up she is, and suddenly the pencil breaks, startling her.

"I'll contact the group and let them know your decision."

They each hang up the phone without another word.

ELEVEN

A projector provides the only light in the rear of a dark room filled with agents recruited for the mission. Joe sits next to Christina.

Gerard, mid-fifties, and Marie, late thirties, both French, explain the mission. The screen behind them shows some of the original cartel members as well as the statistics being referred to. Gerard steps up to the podium and begins.

"It is common knowledge that during World War II the Nazis met with American industrialists to discuss forming a cartel in order to seize and share over one billion dollars in gold as well as famous artwork. But that is only the beginning of the story."

Marie takes over the introduction. "It was at this meeting that a scientist from Germany, Hans Volken, explained to the group a way to control the entire population within fifty to seventy-five years."

On the screen is black-and-white war footage showing Nazis in uniform shaking hands with well-known American industrialists in front of the Waldorf Astoria. Marie continues.

"The first stage involved the use of what would appear to be harmless drugs. The Nazis would be the research arm while the Americans would be the money and marketing arm of the cartel."

There are a variety of reactions from those gathered in the room as Gerard continues.

"In the '40s, German psychologist Kurt Lewin stated that people could be socially and psychologically manipulated in such a way that they would be willing to give up their very souls."

Gerard points to the screen, where the agents are shown footage of Nazis performing psychological experiments on Jewish prisoners. Some "patients" are being hypnotized. Some are being subjected to a strobe light torture. Others are being drugged. A patient screams in agony as he receives electroshock treatments.

"Later Lewin worked for the OSS. The cover was a concern for the moral and spiritual defense of the nation. Between 1949 and 1960 there was wide public acceptance of prescribed drugs such as thorazine, valium--known as Mother's little helper--benzodiazepines, and the world-renowned speed shot to enhance mental capacity pioneered by Max Jacobson, also known as Dr. Feelgood. All of this was and continues to be part of their plan to eventually rule the planet."

Joe listens intently. The screen shows a lobbyist giving a well-received speech to Congress. Marie shakes her head as she points to Lewin--the same face now fills the screen.

"Between 1957 and 1963 Lewin was the key lobbyist and head of the National Institute of Mental Health, NIMH. He devised a master plan that involved influencing the United States Congress to pour billions of government dollars into psychiatric drugs. He was extremely successful. Grants from NIMH increased 870%. In Finland between 1958 and 1967, prescribed hypnotics rose 53% while psychotropic prescriptions rose an amazing 3500%."

The screen now shows a 1963 Ladies Home Journal report. Christina looks over at Joe, who is completely fixated on the presentation.

"In 1963, the Ladies Home Journal reported 1 out of 6 Americans use pills to alter mental attitudes and perceptions. In 1967, a study showed 48% of all adults in the US have taken a psychotropic drug. Sweden reported in 1968 that benzodiazepines accounted for 9.2% of money spent on prescribed drugs. Here in the US, 134 million prescriptions were filled for hypnotic sedatives, antidepressants, and tranquilizers by 1977."

She pauses to let the numbers sink in. The screen next shows a room with Nazi nurses and small children. The children appear zombie-like, withdrawn, and scared. It is obvious Marie is disgusted by what she is reporting.

"In a single year, two antidepressant drugs accounted for half a million prescriptions filled for children between the ages of five and ten."

Joe and Christina look at each other in horror. Gerard continues with the lecture.

"Their ultimate plan was to control the lives of everyone in order to manipulate, but more importantly, design behavior as they saw fit. The mission statement, if you will, is in the name of better mental health and to protect our children. Sound familiar?"

As Gerard says this, the screen shows a scalpel cutting into a man's neck as a chip is pushed under the skin.

"All this was part of their master plan to implant small chips in every person on earth."

An agent reacts by rubbing his neck. Everyone in the room is squirming in their seats.

"They have begun a strong propaganda campaign to convince parents that the abduction of children will become a thing of the past. It also would give them total control of all human functions."

More insidious images appear on the screen showing people laughing and people crying. The last images are of a woman screaming from hallucinations as SS officers look on and laugh.

"They will be able to shock you, make you laugh, make you cry, and make you have hallucinations. By the way, this hypothetical chip has been fully developed and we believe is operational or very close to it. Lights, please."

The lights come on dimly. The group stirs uneasily.

"We have assembled this elite group to dismantle the cartel. It is not going to be easy since we do not know who all their leaders are. I am now going to turn this briefing over to your mission leader."

A tall, handsome man in his mid-sixties stands up and walks to the front of the room. He stands there for a moment looking at the group. He is a strong man with a commanding presence. All business, he is dressed casually elegant. Standing stoically at the front of the room, he eyes his captivated audience like an eagle. He draws a deep breath and begins.

"My name is Surgeon. I am your command leader. This operation is called Switchblade. The sealed packages in front of you contain your new identities as well as codes for communications. These codes are to be memorized and the paper copy destroyed before you leave this room. Each of you has a unique code, and it is not to be shared with your fellow ops. Violation of this direct order will result in your immediate erasure. You also have a secured line if you need to reach me. Let me make this perfectly clear. The infiltration of the cartel goes deep within the Defense Department, CIA, Interpol, and all other global intelligent agencies. We will be going into top secret facilities to purge the databases and..."

In a separate room is a high-tech listening device attached to a recorder, taping the meeting. How can the cartel possibly have known when and where such a meeting was going to take place, unless there is a mole? It would seem to be impossible since this group was handpicked by the very best and most loyal commanders. Screening was brutal. Is the cartel that good? Or is the intelligence world losing the battle? Back in the room, Surgeon continues.

"We will compile a list of all the people involved. Then we need to do some housecleaning. Each name on this list and each complex must be sterilized, with no trace left of it ever having existed. Do not trust anyone outside this room. If anyone wants out, now is the time. Anyone?"

He looks around and no one flinches. His eyes settle on Joe, who momentarily becomes very self-conscience.

"Good." Now open your dossiers and let's begin. Our first target area is Berlin, where it all began."

Surgeon paints such a vivid picture of the account that everyone in the room feels as if they had witnessed it firsthand. At the conclusion of the meeting, agents are paired and given their assignments and last-minute verbal instructions. Joe and Christina are assigned to a high-tech underground security facility in Germany where there is supposed to be an announcement about the chip. They are to leave immediately.

TWELVE

A hand touches a lighted pad, activating a palm scanner. A retina scanner verifies the identity. From overhead a beam covers the entire body. A monitor displays a genomic analysis, the circulatory system, and any identifying marks of the person being scanned. As the scan wraps up, there is a loud click as a three-foot-thick steel door unlocks. Laser beams shut off as the door swings open.

Joe and Christina are standing there waiting to enter. They are undercover, their mission in full swing. They are led to a state-of-the-art tube-like elevator and ushered inside as the vacuum door closes behind them.

"Strap yourselves in tightly," a voice announces. A light goes from red to green. There is a whining sound, and the tube is pressurized. They are rocketed downward.

As they cruise along at breakneck speed Christina says to Joe, "D... D... Did I ev... v... v... ver t... t... tell you I ha... a... ate spe... spe... speeding objects?"

As suddenly as they started, they come to a stop, and they exit the tube. Directly in front of them is a control room monitoring all ongoing global satellite and spy missions. Draped from floor to ceiling is a Nazi flag. They are deep within cartel headquarters.

Joe turns to Christina, who looks gray in the face. "That was fun. Try again?"

"You're sick, Joe."

As they step forward, their bodies are scanned again, revealing their pumping hearts and the blood flowing through their veins. When the scan is complete, they are permitted access to the room. Immediately an SS officer, dressed in a futuristic Nazi uniform, approaches them.

"Papers, please."

They hand over their papers. The officer takes them and disappears into an adjoining room, from which Joe and Christina are being monitored. After a moment the officer returns.

"Here are your access passes. Is there an area of the complex that you wish to be escorted to?"

"Is there a map of the facility?" asks Christina.

As if anticipating the question he promptly pulls a map out of his coat pocket and hands it to Christina. He leaves.

Joe leans toward her. "You won him over. Perhaps he would like to join us for dinner."

"Do I detect a sense of humor?"

"No--fear."

Joe and Christina walk through various rooms. One room in particular draws their attention. The sign next to the door reads: Global Links. Entering the room, they recognize representatives from world terrorist organizations, top military personnel, and government intelligence agencies. The lights dim.

"Good afternoon, ladies and gentlemen. With our latest redesigned chip, Operation Blue Chip is fully functional. You have all been made aware of its capabilities and are obviously here for a demonstration and to purchase our technology."

Gesturing to the standing room only crowd he continues. "It is here that all chips will be monitored and controlled according to your specific instructions and needs. Small beta groups are currently testing our chip to track abducted children. With our help, implementation, and control of the chip's functions, every child in our test groups has been found and reunited with their parents. It is very touching, despite the fact we were the abductors."

Smiles and acknowledgements from those in attendance testify to their warped mindset.

"Once there is global acceptance of our chip, we will be able to track anyone anywhere on Earth. Any non-compliance with our New World government will mean pain, suffering, or even termination. What we have here is the culmination of almost fifty years of research on mind control begun by our founding father."

At that point a portrait of Adolf Hitler is unveiled. The lights come on. Joe and Christina look at each other. The announcer continues.

"We currently have two operational facilities. Most of you know about the one under the North Pole glacier. Additionally, we have developed and built our own space station. It is located behind the moon in a perfect synchronized orbit so that it will remain undetected. Our station is fully armed with state-of-the-art defense technology. I have been authorized to reveal our latest development. Our medical team has cracked the riddle of immortality."

Everyone is stunned. Murmurs ripple through the room. Joe and Christina trade disbelieving glances. The announcer continues once the room settles back down.

"We have developed the perfect clone capable of accepting brain transplants. This is a historic and unprecedented achievement. It means that you can be thirty years young forever. Or can choose to stay the way you are, be younger if you like, or take a different body to change your identity completely. I don't need to explain the staggering implications of this. Visits to either of the stations can be arranged through operations. The chip will be available to the highest bidder from each country. And as previously mentioned, it is from this facility that all chips will be monitored and controlled. The bidding will open at one hundred million dollars. In the meantime, enjoy the rest of your stay. You are free to visit any part of the facility."

The announcer leaves the podium. There are murmurs throughout the room. Joe and Christina walk around the facility. Joe notices a quiet room with wall-to-wall computers and some equipment that looks like it came from the future. He looks at Christina.

"Right," he says as he opens the door. "After you."

They enter the room and begin to examine the equipment. Joe sees a link port.

"Look at this."

Christina goes over to him. "It looks like a Z2 H78A terminal hookup."

Joe wastes no time. "I'll hook in with the remote. Keep an eye peeled."

Christina watches as Joe takes his cell phone and removes the back. A miniature cable comes out and he plugs it into the terminal link. He enters his special code, and the cell phone begins to blink.

Joe smiles at Christina. "We have an uplink."

A wall panel slides open, and two people walk out. Joe turns around to face them while hiding the phone behind his back. Drago and Codie, late twenties, dressed in futuristic military uniforms with swastikas on their arms, enter the room. Drago addresses them.

"Oh, hello. Fascinating room, isn't it?"

Christina turns on the charm. "Yes, fascinating. All this equipment is very impressive."

Trying to buy some time for Joe, Christina walks over to a piece of equipment. Drago and Codie follow her.

"What does this do?"

Joe attempts to disconnect the uplink before he is detected. His fingers search for the connection point. Codie is obviously swayed by Christina's beauty and charm.

"This is command central for the entire operation. It connects to each facility."

Joe continues to struggle with the connection, which is now snagged. Beads of sweat form on his hand, making things even more difficult. Drago begins to walk toward Joe. Their eyes are locked. Joe's fingers slip off the coupling from the sweat. His fingers desperately struggle to regain the process. Drago is now a few feet away. Joe is pinned, and it's all he can do to not give himself away. Drago stops in front of Joe and glares at him with the icy stare of an executioner.

"Excuse me, what is this here?" Christina asks in a loud voice as she reaches for a button.

She distracts Drago, who goes over to her and grabs her hand.

"Please do not touch anything in here. You must first be cleared to access any information from this equipment."

"Sorry," she says.

He is neither moved nor bothered by her good looks, however she has bought Joe a few precious seconds. He continues to work at the connection. Drago turns his attention back to Joe and marches over to him. He stops directly in front of Joe. They stand there nose to nose for what seems like an eternity. Finally, Drago extends his hand.

"I have not met you. My name is Drago. I am head of security for this facility."

The cable silently self-winds back into his cell phone as Joe extends his hand.

"The name is Joe. This is Christina. We are with Contrex Corporation."

They shake hands, like two heavyweight boxers right before a title match. "Drago, we have to finish our rounds," Codie says, breaking the tension.

"Good to meet you both." He turns to Christina. "And please, remember not to touch anything in here."

"Actually, we're leaving too. Joe? Shall we?

"After you."

They leave the room under the watchful eyes of Drago and Codie. As soon as they are clear Christina turns to Joe.

"What the hell were you doing in there?"

"Let's just say I work better when I can see what I'm doing."

Christina looks at him uncertainly. Before she can ask another question, Joe changes the subject.

"I think it is time to leave this party and return to Santa and his merry elves."

"Your codes or mine?" She cruises gracefully past Joe and gives him a seductive smirk.

Butterflies have such a blissful existence. One day you spin yourself to sleep as a caterpillar and before long you're waking up and flying away as a beautiful creature of freedom. Christina is lost in thought as she sits on the hood of the car watching a colorful butterfly flutter hypnotically. She is glad to be out of the facility and breathing fresh country air. She is humming unselfconsciously when Joe emerges from behind a tree. She gives him an innocent smile of contentment. She asks in a soft voice, "Did your codes work okay?"

"I thought we weren't supposed to talk about that to anyone?" Joe says.

"I'm not just anyone."

"Sounds like what the spider said to the fly right before she ate him."

"Thought has crossed my mind," she replies, looking up at him and batting her eyelids.

"Actually, I can trust you. I was on a secret mission behind that tree."

Christina looks at him suspiciously. Her peaceful world of butterflies and pastel colors dispels, returning her to reality. Joe laughs, gets in the car, and turns the engine on.

"I took a pee."

She gets into the passenger seat, and they drive off. "Tell me the story about the spider again."

THIRTEEN

Inside operations, fellow operatives Rachel, Greg McCutchen, Sal, Luis, Soren, and Musky join Joe, Christina, and Surgeon in a darkened room. Surgeon is leading the group.

"Okay, Joe, let's see what you managed to get for us."

Joe goes over to a computer and types in his personal code, and a hologram appears. It shows the precise location of the two facilities. All safe access routes to the glacier are clearly marked. Eventually the hologram begins detailing the space station. Just as the image of the station begins to take on a three-dimensional shape, the hologram disappears. Clearly everyone is disappointed.

"Did you know about the station behind the moon?" asks Christina.

"Yes."

Joe is confused. "Why weren't any of us told?"

"We needed to be sure we had reliable information. This confirms it. Good job, you two."

"Do you have schematics of the station?" asks Greg, who is smoking like a chimney.

"No. We were hoping that Joe and Christina could get them."

"Now what?" asks Soren.

"We go to level two. We begin erasure."

A hologram comes on displaying photos of three people.

"These are our main targets at that facility. Your individual assignments are in the packages before you. See you all at zero four hundred."

Greg McCutchen is in a hotel room smoking one cigarette after another. He is pacing back and forth trying to remain calm. Sweat beads on his forehead. He takes out a handkerchief and wipes it away roughly, tossing the handkerchief on the floor. Looking at it lying there, he picks it up and puts it back in his jacket pocket. After finishing three smokes in a row, he takes a deep breath and erupts in a fit of coughing. It is a deep smoker's cough filled with phlegm. He covers his mouth with the handkerchief, stifling his cough. He then pulls out a cellular phone and dials a number. The other party picks up. Before the party has a chance to say a word, Greg begins talking.

"Let me speak to Widow."

He lights another cigarette as he waits.

"Hello. What information do you have?" comes a voice on the other end of the phone.

This is the moment Greg has been waiting for. If he plays his cards right, he will be set up for life. If he is wrong, the agency may discover he is selling them out. To himself he rationalizes his actions, clinging to the assurance the agency has never done anything for him. After all, didn't the highest bidder always get the most information? Let's hear it for free enterprise, the American Way, Capitalism at its finest! Greg clears his mind and refocuses on his goal: the payoff.

Greg grips the receiver firmly and speaks slowly. "There are two agents assigned to the Pole facility. I'm not sure what their specific assignment is because our orders are sealed."

From across the street in another building a rifleman with a high-powered scope rifle is looking through Greg's window and has Greg in the crosshairs. As the rifleman makes fine adjustments to the scope it becomes time for Greg to make his play.

"Widow, I think it's time to raise the stakes."

"Meaning?"

"I want in."

Widow is sitting in her study, which is replete with books and Old-World carved wood. There is an ornate fireplace and artwork that would rival that found in the world's finest galleries. Sun pierces the sheer curtains, casting shards of light around the room. Every piece of furniture and every knickknack has been thoughtfully and meticulously placed. Not a speck of dust can be seen. Widow's black-gloved hand sets a cigarette in an ashtray.

"What exactly do you want?"

She took the bait, he thinks to himself. "I want to know the entire operation and I want a piece of it. After all, I am your number one mole."

Widow's chair turns to a computer and she types in one word: Terminate.

The rifleman looks at a laptop computer that is signaling him with a low beep. Widow's message blinks on the screen. He loads the chamber with a single large-caliber round and screws on a silencer.

"Greg, you make sense. You are my number one mole in this operation, and for that you deserve accolades."

"I'm glad you see it that way." Greg lights a cigarette and walks over to the window wearing a satisfied smile. Smoke swirls around his face as he draws deeply on his cigarette. He thinks to himself that he has finally entered the big time. He is now a player.

The rifleman's crosshairs are now focused on Greg's forehead. His finger curls around the trigger.

"All right, Greg, you are in. Now, the first thing I need for you to do is look over at the tenth floor of the building across the street. Do you see the window?"

Greg looks over at the building, squinting from the glaring sun.

"Yes, but why?"

"It is one of our safe houses. You will get your assignment there."

Greg smiles, convinced Widow has bought his bluff. The gunman's finger squeezes the trigger. Greg looks hard at the window. A glint from the scope flashes. Greg's expression turns to fear. His CIA training comes crashing into reality, but it is too late.

"Goodbye, Greg," says Widow as she hangs up the phone.

The bullet spins as it emerges from the rifle barrel, heading with precision toward its target. The hot lead begins to expand in its relentless telemetry. Vapor trails tail from the deadly projectile.

Greg's cigarette falls from his mouth. He screams and turns to run. Time slows to a snail's pace. Greg's veins expand as adrenaline-laden blood cascades through his system. Every detail of his life flashes through his mind, from his childhood, his mom, his first kiss, his wedding, joining the CIA, to his first betrayal of government secrets on behalf of a known terrorist group. Sweat beads fly off his head as he is turning to run.

The bullet comes through the window and enters the back of Greg's head. It crushes the skull and bores through his brain, wiping out every memory of his life one at a time. On its continued and obedient path, the bullet exits through his forehead trailing skull fragments and bits of brain tissue. Frozen in place momentarily, his limp body crumples to the floor. His cigarette lands next to him, still lit, until the spreading pool of his blood extinguishes it, and along with it, his last breath of life.

Greg McCutchen's assassin returns home to the solitude and peace of a modest apartment in a middle-class neighborhood. It is obvious from the sparse furnishings, scattered clothing, and piled high dishes that he lives alone.

His cat, Boomerang, greets him at the door. They head to the kitchen for their evening ritual. After he feeds her, he puts his weapons down on the table and pours a drink. He walks over to the couch and turns on the news. The phone rings.

"Is this a secured line?"

"Yes."

"Your results?"

He takes a long sip of his drink. "Clean erasure with no incriminating trails. How about the wire transfer?"

"Check your account." Widow hangs up the phone.

The gunman goes to his computer and logs onto his bank account. There is an e-mail waiting for him. He double-clicks the message. It reads:

Thanks for a job well done. Sorry about the mess in your apartment.

The gunman looks up from the computer. "Shit!"

He grabs Boomerang and makes a mad dash for the door. He grabs the knob and turns it in desperation. He gets the door open, but it's too late. The room erupts in a violent explosion. The entire side of the building explodes, disintegrating almost instantly into small pieces of flying concrete and steel. A ball of flame shoots across the street, almost setting fire to the adjacent building.

Widow's terminal reads, Link terminated, Reconnect, Y/N? Widow's finger taps the 'N' key and then shuts off the computer. She takes an envelope with an official-looking seal and hands it to the man standing in front of her.

"You have your instructions. We do not know who the agents are because one of our moles... Let's just say he is not of his right mind."

The man leaves the room. Widow's hand places a lit cigarette in the ashtray. She pushes a series of buttons and a side wall opens. On a large monitor inside the hidden room is a space station. An officer comes on screen.

"Commander Eli here."

"Commander, what is the status of our new clones?"

"The prototype is ready to be tested."

"Whose brain will be implanted?"

"One of our dedicated agents has volunteered for the test. If successful, he will extend his life by at least fifty years."

"What about reprogramming his mind?"

"Doctor Luctac is ready to proceed."

"Excellent. I will be on the station within a week."

She terminates the connection and hits another button, and the North Pole facility comes on the screen. In his late sixties, Dr. Luctac, surrounded by space-age equipment, is working at a bench. At a quick glance he could be mistaken for Einstein's brother. He looks up and smiles and walks toward the monitor.

"I have good news for you." He goes to his bench and pokes around before finally holding up a chip. "It is finished."

"With all the new features?" Widow asks with thinly veiled excitement.

"Yes, it has an imperceptible release of DGTB 666. As the subject continues to receive this drug, we can start to program at our discretion."

"And if the subject doesn't respond to our programming?"

"Oh, I don't think we will have to worry about that. Take a look at this." A dummy sits in a chair behind explosion-proof glass. "We have implanted the device in its head. It's yours to test."

Widow's hand reaches over and pushes a button. The dummy's head enlarges then explodes. Widow cannot conceal her excitement. "Congratulations! How soon will they be ready?"

"In one to two weeks we will have 13 million ready to ship."

"Thank you, doctor."

Widow shuts off the computer and the wall closes. A flint is struck, igniting a flame that is put to the tip of a cigarette. All loose ends have been neatly and thoroughly tied up.

FOURTEEN

A high-tech sub glides silently through the iceberg-laden water. The massive size of the icebergs is a clear sign that the sub is under the North Pole region.

The outer shell of the sub is fitted with multiple series of propellers, which have an outer casing with steering flaps attached. The sub's unprecedented jet engines provide the sub with silent underwater movement.

As it glides through the icy waters, the newly redesigned swastika is clearly visible on the tailpiece. The destination for this unclassified sub is the North Pole Glacier Facility. The bridge is alive with activity, with the captain calling out orders.

"Rotate the propellers and prepare to take us up to 150 feet."

"Aye-aye, captain. Bubble coming to 150 feet," barks back the navigator.

"Slow us to docking speed and inform our guests we are here."

A seaman acknowledges the captain's orders and disappears. As the sub continues on course, it is also being viewed on a holographic screen at Operation Switchblade's headquarters by Surgeon and a few members of the team.

"It is true then. They have developed their high-speed sub. Amazing. We must find a way to... borrow it." Surgeon turns to the others. "Greg McCutchen has been assassinated. We have good reason to suspect he was a mole. The bullet was German-issued secret intelligence caliber. His last call was untraceable, and he was not using his specific coded sequences."

"Is our operation at risk?" asks Sal.

"Good question. I'm not sure yet. We have to find out who the trigger guy was and trace him back to the source." After a brief moment of silence Surgeon continues. "Sal, Luis, I'm sending you as backup to the North Pole Facility. Joe and Christina don't know this yet. I will send Joe a message to expect a package. Remember that they are there to eliminate the facility and everyone inside of it. You two are to make sure that no one except Joe and Christina gets off that iceberg alive. Any questions?" Headshakes all around. "Good. You leave now."

Christina closes a lighter and draws deeply on her cigarette. Along with Joe and some other passengers she stands in a large submarine docking area. Several other subs are also docked. The sheer size of the place is staggering. Joe looks at Christina.

"I didn't know you smoke?"

"I don't that often."

"You just happen to be carrying cigarettes and a lighter?"

Christina looks at him. There seems to be an uncomfortable moment between them. Joe is about to say something when an attendant approaches them.

"You have each been assigned a guest suite while you are staying with us. If you will follow me I will take you to your rooms."

The group follows the attendant.

The accommodations include all the customary creature comforts. Joe unpacks his carry-on laptop and begins to type.

Dear Jimmy,

Arrived safely but reporting more ice than expected at the North Pole.

The North Pole Facility's Operations Room is lined with glass walls affording a view of a wide variety of sea life. The rest of the room is filled floor to ceiling with equipment. An orderly dressed in a military uniform notices something on his monitor.

"Sir, there is a cellular transmission link underway."

Hans Stroyer, early forties, is physically superior to most men alive. His face looks like it has been chiseled out of granite. With a stone-cold expression that gives absolutely nothing away, he projects an aura of utter intimidation.

"Where did it originate and where is it going?"

The orderly is typing on his keyboard as fast as he can.

"I'm not sure, but whoever it is has some very sophisticated equipment."

"Can you intercept the message?"

"Maybe." Sensing that maybe isn't good enough, he continues working at a feverish pace. "Shit, this guy is really good. His scramble is in the range of..."

As he says this, Hans puts his large hand on the orderly's shoulder. "Spare me the details. Just get me the message--now."

"Yes, sir."

While Joe is at work on his computer there is a loud knock at the door. He quickly powers down and cautiously approaches the door and unlocks it. As the door opens Joe takes a step backwards.

"Hello, sir, I have your luggage," says the assistant standing there.

With a sense of relief, Joe says, "Thank you. Please set it over there."

The assistant puts down Joe's bags and is about to leave when he stops, turns, and reaches into his jacket. Joe is frozen. He thinks this is it--he has been discovered and is either going to be terminated where he stands or taken for interrogation. Between the two, Joe would prefer that it end painlessly now.

"Oh yes, I almost forgot. This came for you." He pulls out an envelope and hands it to Joe, then leaves.

Inside the operations room of the station, the orderly's screen stops dead. He looks up at Hans.

"The link has been broken. We got nothing."

Hans is visibly angry.

Unaware of how close he was to being discovered; Joe opens the envelope.

It reads:

Dear Joe:

Your girlfriend is not who she appears to be. I'm concerned for your safety. Do not trust her. The man who gave you this letter is a trusted friend. We still have some people inside. Be careful.

Love, Mom.

Joe looks up, his face a mask of sheer confusion. Christina a double agent? This isn't happening, he thinks to himself. In an instant, all events leading up to his recruitment flood his mind. He begins trying to piece the puzzle together. He thinks about how convenient it was that she had such a high clearance level. Could the group he was recruited into be part of a master plan or is he being played by the cartel? He rereads the note from his mother, then he lights the paper on fire and watches it until the ashes scatter into unrecognizable carbon bits.

The flowers in Christina's room seem lonely and out of place. They are vibrant in color and their delicate fragrance permeates the room. Holding them in her hands, she is reminded of when she was a kid visiting her grandparents' house. How she loved playing in the brook and running up the heavily wooded paths to the meadow. Her memory leads her to laughter and eventually to screams as she and her childhood friends are terrorized by a bumblebee. Christina's face relaxes into a smile as she recalls when the family would gather together late at night and listen to her grandfather play a three-finger picking banjo. like a world-class picker. He was a farmer with a big heart who played his banjo out of a love of music and his family. She can still see him--

tall and elegant and proudly playing and singing with all his heart. They were poor, but rich when it came to family and home life.

Christina puts the flowers back in the vase and sits down to type a message at her computer. Her reverie behind her, she turns her attention bank to her mission. Without warning, the door to her room opens. Instinctively she shuts off the computer. Turning around, she sees Joe standing there.

"Aren't you supposed to--"

"I want answers."

"About what?"

"Who do you really work for?"

"What are you talking about?"

"How did you know my mother is alive?"

"I told you, the group gave me that information to gain your trust."

"Really? It was about trust?"

"You know that."

"Okay, then trust me."

"I do, Joe."

"Prove it. What are your code numbers?"

"You're asking the impossible."

"I thought the group was about trust, Christina."

She doesn't respond to his push.

"Are we all on our own or is there something else the group hasn't told me?

"Like what?"

"If this operation is so vital to the world's security, then why is only a handful of people involved? How come we have totally extracted ourselves from the system to run this operation? And when do we get to reenter the system as real people again?"

Christina looks at Joe and turns away. "Soliciting outside help could lead to a security breech. We had to disappear so we could never be traced back to operations." She pauses and looks directly into his searching eyes. "And we will never reenter the system."

"What the hell does that mean?"

"Our true identities have been permanently erased. Joe, we no longer exist. We are in effect the world's unofficial secret government without official support."

"Why wasn't I told this before joining?"

"Would you still have joined? Joe, it was your family who started this by discovering the information during World War II. These people murdered your father and tried to murder your mother. You owe it to your family to carry on with this work."

"Don't talk to me about responsibility. Now tell me why we are all segregated in this operation."

"If there is an internal leak or a mole, it would stop there. We now know it works--or Greg McCutchen would still be alive and selling us out. Without any of us knowing the entire scope the group cannot be stopped in its efforts. Yes, we are alone, but we are also together."

"If that's so, who were you talking with on the secured line?"

"I was about to report to Surgeon when you came bursting into the room. I terminated the link."

She goes over and tries to comfort him, rubbing his shoulders and kissing his neck. Joe shrugs her off.

"Isn't this how it all started in the first place... to get me involved?"

Christina slaps him across the face. "You ungrateful bastard. How dare you! Yes, it was my job to recruit you, but things have changed. Now you have to trust the group."

"How can any of us have trust when we are trained to lie and kill?" Joe turns and leaves the room.

Christina is left alone to contend with conflicting emotions. I did my job... I recruited him as ordered... I'm a professional... Stay focused.... He is... I'm not... Her eyes fill with tears.

The door slams shut as Joe begins to pace in his room. Frustrated, he goes to his computer, his mind filled with possibilities but no answers. It is time for the truth. He types on the computer: Have you heard from my traveling partner yet? After a brief wait he receives a response. Not yet. Is everything okay with your accommodations?

He stares at the monitor wondering what to do next. Then he types, Yes, all is well. He shuts off the computer and opens his suitcases. Frustrated, he begins to remove things from secret compartments concealed in the linings and to lay them on the bed. His hands shake with anger.

As the sun rises, the colors of morning dance across the vast expanse of the North Pole. Majestic icebergs dipped in shades of blue rise into the air like crystalline edifices where the gods still dwell. Encased in the ice are mysteries of the planet frozen in time. A bird's eye view of the landscape reveals a manmade iceberg with an above ground facility. On the ice-covered runway are a few aircraft that are capable of space launches from the ground. Guards and maintenance personnel are transporting the machines to their designated positions.

Inside the facility, Dr. Luctac is addressing the group of visitors from his laboratory.

"We have been developing a variety of medical wonders. They range from genetic engineering of animals to our specialty, human cloning and mind control. We have produced rabbits the size of men." He smiles at the spellbound audience members. "As a matter of fact, last night you enjoyed one of our experiments for dinner."

There are murmurs of delight.

"My assistants will show you what I am talking about."

Dr. Luctac turns to his assistants, who go over to a door and unlock it. Christina looks on, wondering to herself why Joe is not there. Had something happened to him? Was his cover blown? At the same time she can't help wondering if he is up to something. Then across the room Joe casually enters through a door and joins the others.

"Where have you been? We were to meet here this morning."

"Just checking out a few things." He turns to her. "You learn anything?"

"I found a way into the main computer room. We can link the entire facility and--"

"Whose codes are we using?"

"We have to use both our codes in sequence or it will not work. You knew that when we were briefed. What's going on, Joe?"

"Let's just say that sometimes things aren't what they appear to be."

Christina doesn't know what he is talking about and stares at him coldly.

"We have exactly five hours to complete our assignment and get the hell out of here."

"Which assignment is that, Christina?" Joe cannot get the letter from his mother out of his mind. It plays over and over in his head. How could he have been so blind?

"Ladies and gentlemen, I am proud to unveil to you the results of our genetic experimentation," announces Dr. Luctac.

No one is prepared for what happens next. Through the open door comes a rabbit that is almost seven feet tall. Gasps go up from the crowd. Joe and Christina are stunned. Dr. Luctac seeks to quell the uneasiness in the room.

"There is no reason for alarm. This animal is perfectly harmless."

The doctor goes up to the rabbit and strokes its fur. He takes some food out of the pocket of his lab coat, and the rabbit follows him to the door. As the rabbit goes through, the door is closed behind it.

"We have achieved similar results with lobsters, shrimp, clams, turkeys, ducks, and quite a few other animals."

One of the members of the group, Francis Fonzoli, a man in his early forties, stares at Christina. Joe notices this. She turns away from Fonzoli, who turns his attention back to Dr. Luctac as he finishes his presentation.

"How much success have you had with your experiments on mind control, doctor?"

"Ah, Mr. Fonzoli. This is why we are gathered here today. Let's proceed to our medical facility."

Joe asks Christina, "Friend of yours?"

"Never saw him before. Jealous?"

Joe thinks about it for a moment and doesn't comment. The group continues its tour. Joe detours to a work area and palms an object under a table. The device is activated and blinking.

The group accompanies Dr. Luctac through long corridors of metal mesh. It is a sterile environment, where not so much as a mote of dust is tolerated. The lighting is bright enough for the metal walls to give off residual heat. Every ten feet are metal doors that can only be opened with a high clearance pass. At the end of the hall are two armed guards who greet the doctor and his guests.

"Good morning, doctor. Would you please use the palm and retina scan for verification?"

The doctor turns to the group. "As you can see, the security is flawless. No one is above suspicion, and everyone must be cleared each time they enter a high security area. After all, there are bad people out there."

The crowd enjoys a self-conscious laugh. Dr. Luctac passes through the security checkpoint.

The retina scan and palm identification confirms Dr. Luctac's identity. "Good morning, doctor," says a computer-generated voice. The doors open and the guards step aside, allowing the group to enter into the medical laboratory. Inside is a room the likes of which none of them has ever seen. Dr. Luctac is greeted by his two assistants.

"We are ready, doctor."

"Very well." The doctor turns back to the group. "It is in this medical facility that we have perfected the art of mind control."

A series of laser beams safeguarding one of the rooms is shut off. Dr. Luctac's assistants remove a prisoner from a cell.

"Our subject today has committed crimes against the cartel." Doctor Luctac walks over to the prisoner. "Allow me to introduce you all to Agent Lyle."

Agent Lyle is a strong, handsome man in his mid-thirties. He stands emotionless before the viewing audience. He is in fact one of Great Britain's best-trained secret agents. In the course of a mission conducted on behalf of his government, he inadvertently uncovered a paper trail that led back to the cartel. The cartel's intelligence section uncovered his true identity and brought him in for interrogation. When the interrogation proved futile he was turned over to the doctor as a subject for his studies on mind control.

"As you can imagine, Agent Lyle is a very difficult person to control." Luctac nods to his assistants, who bend Agent Lyle's head forward, exposing a small incision on the back of his neck.

"As you can see, our chip has been inserted in him. It is a painless insertion and can be done with local anesthetic, provided the patient cooperates."

The doctor smiles sadistically as he anticipates what he hopes will come next. He turns to Agent Lyle and examines the incision.

"Thanks to the implant--along with some of my personal touches--Agent Lyle's mind has been reprogrammed."

Elise Monroe, a scientist in her late thirties, looks up from taking notes. "Dr. Luctac, what exactly makes the subject responsive?"

"Excellent question, Elise. We have developed a drug that puts the subject in a state much like that of a child--innocent and without any frame of reference."

As Dr. Luctac continues to explain, Elise Monroe and Joe make eye contact. Christina notices.

"Friend of yours?"

"Never saw her before. Jealous?"

Christina eyes Elise like a cat ready to pounce on its prey.

"Over the past fifty years," continues Dr. Luctac, "we have introduced to the public such 'harmless' drugs such as Prozac, Valium, diet pills, hair growth remedies, and other chemically based products. Within the complex compounds and links, we have discovered that the brain is capable of releasing an unclassifiable liquid that reacts with our drugs to make the subject more readily programmable. Please observe."

The assistants lower the lasers in another cell. They walk another prisoner out to the center of the room and sit him in a chair. He is in shackles.

"Our next subject has not been programmed since we no longer have any need for him. He is a civilian.

The subject is screaming at the top of his lungs. "WHO ARE YOU PEOPLE? WHERE AM I? I WANT MY LAWYER."

"This doesn't feel right, Joe."

"We cannot interfere no matter what. Understand?" Joe says in a calm, controlled voice.

Christina looks at Joe, not knowing what to do but needing to do something.

Dr. Luctac hands Agent Lyle a gun. Some in the audience grow nervous.

"I assure you there is nothing to worry about. Our agent friend is completely under our control." He turns to the agent. "Good morning, Mr. Lyle."

Agent Lyle speaks in a normal tone and appears to be in control of all his faculties.

"Good morning, doctor."

"Do you know this man?"

"I have never seen him before. Who is he?"

Dr. Luctac turns his attention back to the audience. "As you can see, Agent Lyle does not appear to be under the influence of drugs or any other type of control. He is not zombie-like. Part of our success is retaining our subjects' ability to function in everyday life until we need them." He turns to Lyle. "Mr. Lyle, do you have a wife?"

"Yes, and two small children. Do you want to see a picture of them?"

The group laughs.

"Not right now."

Dr. Luctac pulls out a piece of paper.

"Mr. Lyle, I have just been informed that this man has been convicted of murder."

The civilian's head pops up. "Murder? What the hell are you saying? I didn't murder anyone. Get me my lawyer--now. I have rights."

"Did you hear that, Mr. Lyle? He murdered someone and thinks he has rights."

"I heard him, Dr. Luctac."

Agent Lyle's personality begins to change with each subtle push from Dr. Luctac. Doctor Luctac signals to one of his assistants, who goes over to a panel and begins to key in a numbered sequence.

"What my assistant is administering is a neurological electronic signal which triggers a large dose of our formula. In doing this, our subject's programming becomes very active and quite responsive. Observe. Mr. Lyle, do you know anything about the trial?"

"No, doctor." Lyle stares at the civilian.

"Mr. Lyle, he murdered a woman."

Lyle's expression begins to harden. He begins to grind his teeth. His face twitches. He continues to stare at the civilian with ice in his eyes.

"You murdered a woman? You're a coward."

"Listen, pal, these people are crazy. I never killed anyone."

Christina looks at Joe. She knows what's coming and feels completely helpless. Her hands are clenched tight. Joe nudges her and gives her a warning look so she'll stay focused.

"Mr. Lyle, not only did this man kill a woman, but he also killed her two children."

Lyle's eyes are bulging from his head. He is breathing very hard. Beads of sweat are forming on his forehead. His body begins to quiver from the adrenaline flowing through his veins. Dr. Luctac signals to his assistant, who talks into a microphone.

"Lyle, do you hear me?"

He whispers, "I hear you."

"This man is wanted by the FBI for murdering a woman and two children. He is an escaped prisoner and is running from the law."

Lyle turns his head sideways in a contorted way. He is clearly out of his mind. With complete calm, Dr. Luctac looks at his guests like a starving wolf looking at a helpless chicken caught in a wire fence.

"This is my very favorite part." Dr. Luctac signals to his assistant. "Mr. Lyle, the woman's name was Anita."

Lyle lets out a scream.

"The children's names were Sandra and Jimmy. This man murdered Anita, Sandra, and Jimmy, Lyle--your family. You have been assigned to hunt him down. Be careful, he is carrying a weapon." Dr. Luctac turns to his spellbound audience. "Please note that this man doesn't have a weapon, but in Mr. Lyle's mind he is armed and dangerous."

Dr. Luctac nods to his assistant, who turns on a recording device. There are the sounds of Lyle's family playing and laughing as Lyle strains to hear them. Tears well in his eyes. The recording stops at the sounds of gunshots and bodies falling to the floor. A small voice calls out, "Mommy, daddy, please help me." Lyle turns on the civilian and raises the gun to the man's head.

"Hey, man... What the hell are you doing? Look at me. I don't have a weapon. Come on, snap out of it." The civilian now realizes what is coming and begins to sob. "I didn't kill your family. I swear to God."

"Did you hear him, Lyle? He admits to killing your family."

Lyle's eyes are red and hate-filled. He walks over to the civilian, puts the gun barrel to the man's head, and pulls the trigger. Nothing happens. Lyle pulls the trigger several more time and still nothing happens.

Dr. Luctac nods once again to his assistant. "Congratulations, Lyle. The target has been terminated."

Lyle smiles. There is a puddle under the chair of the civilian. Realizing he is still alive, the man laughs with intense relief, on the verge of vomiting. Recovering a bit, the civilian becomes mad. "ARE YOU ALL NUTS?" Doctor Luctac remains calm.

"Please escort our prisoner back to his cell."

The second assistant complies. As they walk toward the cell, Dr. Luctac nods at his other assistant, who whispers something in the microphone. Lyle begins to walk toward the prisoner. As Lyle approaches, he pulls a wire out of his pocket. Just as they reach the cell opening, he slips the wire around the civilian's neck. The civilian grapples for the wire as his feet flail, trying to keep his balance. The choking sounds continue as the civilian struggles for air and life. The two men disappear into the cell. More sounds of death can be heard until it becomes absolutely quiet.

"I will now show you just how powerful our research is." Dr. Luctac nods once again to his assistant, who speaks again in a normal voice into the microphone.

"Mr. Lyle, it is lunch time and you are very hungry. Let's eat."

Lyle comes out of the cell smiling. "Anyone hungry? I'm starving."

The group applauds, except for Christina, who is too shocked to move. Joe gives her another nudge, and she responds by clapping politely.

FIFTEEN

A miniature sub glides silently to a stop alongside the underwater exterior of the North Pole facility. A hatch opens and two divers enter the water and swim into an open tube. Inside the sub docking station two divers emerge from the blackness of the water--agents Sal and Luis. They climb out of the water, each carrying a case, and quickly stow their gear under some crates. Stripping off their wetsuits, they depart the docking area. As they turn a corner they come face to face with an ominous-looking weapon pointed at their heads.

"That is far enough," the guard says.

Sal begins to talk to the soldier. As he does, Luis slips a throwing star out from under his sleeve.

"What's the problem?"

"What are you two doing in here?"

"Fixing the sub."

"I wasn't told anything about a problem with one of the subs. What's in the cases?"

"Our tools."

"Open them."

As Sal squats down to open the cases the soldier steps closer to see what's inside. The soldier looks down inside the first case. In a fluid movement Luis throws the star and strikes the soldier in his throat. The soldier drops his weapon and clutches at his throat. Luis draws a knife and finishes the job. They drag the body out of sight, gather their cases, and move on to their next position.

Christina is in her room, in the throes of a restless sleep. The sheet covering her is ajar, exposing most of her thigh. As her eyes flit back and forth behind her eyelids, a hand covers her mouth. Startled, she tries to defend herself but has been caught unawares. She opens her eyes and recognizes Sal, who is flanked by Luis. Once she calms down, Sal removes his hand.

"Shit, you nearly gave me a heart attack. What are you two doing here--and where's Joe?"

Luis can't help but notice her body. She sees him staring at her and covers herself up. Still embarrassed, he focuses on the mission again.

"Did Joe plant the device in the communications room?"

"Yes. Watch the door so I can get dressed."

She motions for them to turn around, which they both do, reluctantly.

"Hurry, we don't have a lot of time."

Once Christina is dressed the three of them move out, doing their best to avoid detection.

From inside the security room, the three of them are spotted on a monitor as they make their way down a hallway. A hand grabs a submachine-gun and leaves the room as Christina, Sal, and Luis move cautiously around a corner. Luis brings the group to a halt.

"Okay, I'll go get Joe while you two start the setup."

From behind them an authoritative voice commands, "Move and you're all dead. Now one by one slowly get up and turn around."

The three rise one at a time and turn around with hands in the air. It is Joe, and he has a submachine-gun strapped across his chest.

With a conquering smile on his face he says, "Nice of you to join me."

Sal is not amused. "What the hell are you doing?"

Joe points out some concealed cameras.

"Smile. The upload we got didn't give us that spec."

Christina looks at Joe. "What are you doing up?"

"Surgeon sent me a message to expect a package." Joe holds up a remote control. "Now listen up. Once I render the monitoring and communication systems inoperative, we will have ten minutes max before an all-out search is commenced. Christina, you're with Luis, and I will go with Sal."

Each team takes one of the cases.

"Check your watches. Ready and mark." Joe pushes a button on the remote. The lights on the mini cameras go out. "We meet in the sub bay in ten minutes."

The two teams move off in separate directions.

Inside the missile room a vent comes off the wall, and Christina and Luis enter the room. They see rows of missiles stacked in precise military lines. Everything in the room is orderly and immaculate. A huge rocket stands on an interior launch pad, the steam and vapor issuing from the sides indicating a launch is imminent. Luis is taken aback as he absorbs the implication of a "ready" war room.

"Holy shit. I didn't see this coming."

"Me neither. But it will make a terrific fireworks display. Shall we?"

Luis smiles at her and opens the case. He hands Christina a strange looking object.

"Be very careful with these. One slip and we are history. Secure them to the wall and set the timer for ten minutes. Sal has the trigger device to start the countdown."

Christina and Luis start to place the devices. Luis walks up to the launch pad and places one right on the rocket. He pats it.

"Happy birthday, big fellow."

Joe and Sal are in the computer room. Joe works feverishly at one of the computers. "What are you looking for?" Sal asks.

"I'm not sure, but I'm hoping to find a link leading to the top of the cartel here. Then we will be able to identify all the leaders once and for all."

"While you are in there, float me a loan with no interest or payments, would you?"

Joe smiles at Sal. "Dream on. Oh, hello."

"Find something?"

"If I'm not mistaken, these are the medical files for their experiments."

Sal looks over his shoulder.

"Can you uplink them?"

"I think so."

"You keep at it." Sal goes off and begins to place charges under and around all the computer equipment.

Christina and Luis walk down a long hallway, both of them distracted by the construction material. Luis is getting the willies.

"What kind of hallway is this?"

"Beats me. The walls seem alive. This is very weird."

With each step they take the walls undulate and the floor lights up. They come to the end of the hall and find themselves standing in front of a formidable steel door that is twenty feet high and ten feet wide. The door is accessible only by a code. Luis takes out a tiny computer and begins to wire the panel. Christina keeps a watchful eye.

On the other side of the facility, Joe is continuing his computer search when he discovers something.

"Sal, look at this."

Sal comes over.

"This facility has a spacecraft capable of ground launches into space, and it is specifically set for their station on the opposite side of the moon.

"Any way to destroy it?"

"Not sure yet." Joe continues to type commands when suddenly he says, "Bingo."

"Found a way?"

"No, better. I found the personnel files."

"Joe, we have to move on to our next room if we want to live through this mission."

"You start without me. This information is too important to leave behind."

"I'll give you three minutes, and then I'm dragging your ass out of here. Agreed?"

"Agreed."

Unbeknownst to Joe, history seems to be repeating itself. Whereas during WWII his father found the secret room that began his mission, Joe has now found the list of those responsible for the cartel and his father's death, in essence continuing his parents' work where they left off.

As Joe and Sal continue their mission, Luis still struggles with the door. Christina is becoming anxious. Finally he locks in on the codes and the door slides open with a loud hiss. Luis and Christina look at each other, their expressions read like an open book.

Luis stares at what he sees. "Oh, shit."

Behind monitors showing regions of space, the space station, a strategic hit zone on the earth, and an aircraft docking at the station is a team of personnel. The entire room stops work as the doors finish opening and everyone turns to see who has entered.

"Luis, something tells me this was a bad career move."

At that instant, gunshots sound and bullets start to ricochet around the room. Suddenly Christina and Luis are in a fight for their lives. A few men reach inside cabinets and withdraw weapons that are like nothing ever before seen on earth. Three guards power up the weapons.

One of them says, "Let's welcome our guests to the space age, shall we?"

As the fight ensues, a computer-generated voice announces throughout the facility, "Weapons have been discharged. Security alert is now at Level 5."

Laser beams and bullets are flying. Christina jumps behind a workstation. A guard sees her, aims, and fires. A beam strikes the workstation, vaporizing it. Within seconds the workstation is reduced to a fiery ball, exposing Christina. She sees the shooter taking aim to fire again. She dives out of the way, rolls, turns, and shoots, hitting the laser gun directly. It implodes with an electrical charge that engulfs the man. He screams as his body melts into a mound of liquid fire.

Luis picks off soldiers while at the same time placing explosive devices under several desks. He is under a workstation setting a charge when a huge foot comes down on his neck. He looks up to see a man pointing a pistol directly at his forehead.

"Say your prayers, asshole." He cocks the gun and begins to squeeze the trigger. Suddenly he is thrown off Luis as Christina tackles him. They roll around fighting for control of the gun. Christina knows she is no match for him in this fight to the death. Suddenly his pistol discharges, grazing Christina's arm. She rolls over in pain.

"You bastard. You shot me."

The man gets up and aims at her. "Did I hurt you, little girl?"

Christina looks up at him. "Not as bad as I'm about to hurt you."

Christina's foot rockets upwards, landing squarely in the gunman's groin. He doubles over in excruciating pain. She springs up and does a spinning roundhouse kick to the man's face. It twists his head around, snapping his neck, and he falls to the floor dead. Luis runs over to her.

"All the charges are set. Let's get the hell out of here... and thanks, Chris--"

His words are cut short as his eyes go wide. Christina looks on in confusion as Luis falls forward, a knife sticking out of his back. A soldier stands there triumphantly. Christina screams, takes Luis's machine gun, and empties it into the soldier. His body hits the wall with such force that it is suspended there until the last bullet hammers into his chest. The soldier's limp, blood-soaked carcass streaks the wall with crimson smudges as it slides to the floor.

"Luis, I'll get you out of here."

He smiles at her. "Sure you will." His eyes begin to glaze over. "Oh boy, this hurts," he mutters, and they are his last words before he dies.

The nearby strike of a laser beam reminds Christina that her life is still up for grabs. Above her head is a hole left by the beam. It is dripping liquid fire. Christina's eyes fill with a fire of their own. She pulls a hand grenade out of her vest and tosses it up to the catwalk on which the laser gunman is positioned. The explosion sends bodies and body parts flying in all directions and knocks out the last remaining laser gunman. Christina sees the laser and grabs it, shooting her way out of the room as it erupts in a series of terrific explosions. The lights in the facility start to blink, and the computer-generated voice sounds once again over the speaker system.

"Explosions have been detected. Please relocate to the designated shelters until we have containment." The lights continue to flash as the message periodically replays.

Meanwhile, Joe looks at his watch and then back to the computer, where various pictures and dossiers are coming up on the screen. Joe calls over his shoulder.

"Sal, you will not believe what I have here."

Gunfire erupts, and the plate glass windows behind Joe explode in a rain of tiny shards. A body flies through and lands next to Joe. It is Sal. In his hand is the timer, which reads 9 minutes 20 seconds.

"Oh, shit." Joe is about to make a run for it when his communication device signals him.

"Joe, this is Christina, where are you?"

"Computer room. Where are you?"

"I just left the sub dock. The sub has been destroyed and Luis is dead."

"Sal is dead, too."

Joe considers their options. "We have less than nine minutes to get out of here before this iceberg becomes a puddle of water. Meet me at the launch site."

Inside the medical room, Dr. Luctac is frantically gathering papers and downloading data. Elise Monroe has her hands full helping him. The security alert continues.

"Intruders have been detected. All non-essential personnel are expendable."

Joe finds himself running through the lab. Dr. Luctac and Elise look up and see him. Impending doom is written all over his face. He has had enough, and the time has come to take care of business. As Joe crosses the lab toward Dr. Luctac and Elise, a door opens. Dr. Luctac and Elise's faces register relief. Joe turns and sees it is Hans.

Hans addresses Dr. Luctac and Elise. "You two keep working. This will only take a minute." Hans pulls out a gun, Joe dives for safety. He quickly pulls a wire from his watch and attaches it to one side of an opening separating him from Hans. He removes some plastic explosive and attaches it to the other side of the opening. He inserts a small detonator in the plastic and moves quickly away.

Dr. Luctac and Elise confidently carry on their work. "I'm almost finished downloading to the SE2 zip." He turns to Elise. "Have you finished?"

"Almost, doctor."

Elise looks over and sees Joe crawling away from the opening to get the drop on Hans.

"Hey, Hans," she shouts.

Hans looks over at her, and she points in Joe's direction. Hans smiles and moves around to the other side.

"Elise, go over to the board and release Lyle. Give him a voice command to erase our intruder," says Dr. Luctac.

Elise goes over and shuts off the cell's beams while Hans closes in on Joe.

"The longer I take to find you, the more painful your death will be."

As Hans says this, a coin rolls up to his foot. He picks it up and looks at it.

"A gold coin? Are you trying to buy your freedom?" He laughs. "I have more than I'll ever need of this stuff. But thanks anyway. I will keep this as a souvenir of our meeting." He slips it into his pocket. "Now it is time to say goodbye."

Joe's hand comes out from under a workstation holding a remote. Hans appears confused.

"Did you know that gold is a great conductor of electricity?" Joe asks smugly.

Hans quickly realizes that he has been set up and scrambles to get the coin out of his pocket. Joe shows himself.

"What was it you said? Oh yeah: It is time to say goodbye." Joe pushes the button. Hans's body begins jerking like a puppet as a high-voltage electrical charge surges through it. His clothes start to smoke. Hans lets out a strangled, spasmodic scream as he falls to the floor dead. Joe comes out and stands up. A bullet whizzes by, barely missing his head. Joe dives for the floor once again, but not before seeing that Elise is the shooter. He scrambles across the room, hoping that Elise will follow him. Lyle is now out of his cell and appears to be in an oddly jovial mood.

"Is anyone hungry?"

Elise looks at Lyle. "Shut up, you asshole. You see that man?"

"Yes."

"He is the one who killed your family."

Immediately Lyle's smile distorts into the cold face of a hunter lusting for the kill. Joe sees his gun across the room, but there is no way to reach it. It is going to come down to old-fashioned hand-to-hand combat. Joe stands up, takes a deep breath, and readies himself for a battle to the death.

The fight begins when Lyle flings him across the room. Joe gets up, knowing it is going to be all or nothing if he expects to survive. The fight unfolds as Dr. Luctac and Elise continue downloading medical files.

"Elise, there is another computer that needs to be downloaded. Don't worry about Lyle, he will take care of things here."

Elise would rather watch the fight but does as Luctac requests. She starts to type into a computer. "What files do you want to download?"

"The ones labeled PoleFac.Med."

Meanwhile the brutal battle between Lyle and Joe shows no signs of letting up. Elise glances up a few times to see if Joe is dead yet. "Lyle, just kill him."

Dr. Luctac goes over to another part of the room. The facility occasionally shudders as the metal support structure nears critical fatigue.

Joe appears to be all but defeated, and finally Lyle moves in for the kill. As he is about to strike, another tremor ripples through the facility and Lyle is thrown off balance. Joe takes advantage of this and springs to his feet, running for his life. Lyle pursues Joe up onto the overhead rafters. They each pick up a piece of fallen metal debris and use them as swords, clanging them together, igniting sparks. The makeshift swords are heavy and awkward. Both have reached their physical limits. The fight continues as if in slow motion, the two men matching blow for blow. In a supreme show of will, Joe swings his metal object at Lyle, catching him off balance and sending him over the side of the railing.

Lyle's body comes crashing down on top of a computer. Elise screams. She looks around and sees Joe sliding down a pole to the floor. She takes a machine gun off the counter and aims it at Joe. Joe stops dead in his tracks and looks around for a way out, but it is useless; he is trapped.

"Before I kill you, I would like to know who you are."

"Do you even know how to use that thing?" asks Joe sarcastically.

Elise begins to laugh. "Have you ever seen the face of someone who knows that death is inevitable? Well, here is what it looks like."

She points the machine gun at the floor and squeezes the trigger. The barrel spits out bullets, ripping up the floor heading on a collision course toward Joe. The bullets stop within inches of Joe's feet. Elise's face registers shock. She looks down and sees her blouse covered in blood. She drops the gun and falls face down. Standing behind her is Christina, holding a smoking .357 handgun. She runs over to Joe.

"Are you finished playing around?"

"Cute."

Christina sees the doctor making a run for it. She aims at him, ready to do to him what she just did to Elise. Joe grabs Christina and pulls her to the floor. Christina is about to argue with him when the doctor trips the booby trap. The explosion sends pieces of the doctor flying through the air mixed with printouts and SE2 zips.

Joe smiles at Christina. "Did I mention I set a booby trap?"

She surveys the destruction. "What about the links? Are they in place?"

"Yes. Now we have to get to the spacecraft on the launch pad."

As they flee the lab, they each grab an assortment of weapons--just in case. The countdown continues with 2 minutes 12 seconds left. Joe and Christina make their way toward the ship. As the bloody battle continues, bodies fall all around them. They shift positions and run back-to-back, covering each other. Christina sees the spacecraft.

"I think it's time we get into that thing over there."

"It's called a spacecraft, Christina."

"I don't care if it's a jelly donut as long as we can use it for cover."

"Okay, on three. Ready?" She nods her head.

"One, two, three..." They break from their back-to-back position and lay down a barrage of gunfire, sending the soldiers scrambling for cover and buying them the precious seconds it takes for them to run into the spacecraft and close the door. Once inside, Christina looks around.

"Okay, now what?"

"Strap yourself in cause this could get rocky." Joe throws switches with precision, powering up the ship's rockets to full thrust and propelling them off the launch pad. The timer is at 3 seconds as the ship clears the launch pad. The thrust of the takeoff is such that the craft begins to roll over and over.

Christina is looking a bit sickly. "I don't like this."

The timer counts, 2... 1... 0... At the zero mark, each preset device emits a signal connecting all of them to one another. When they are in sync, there ensues a momentary stillness noticed by everyone in the facility. Weapons are lowered in the false sense the battle is over and the invaders have been vanquished. Not even the computer voice can be heard.

A split second later an ear-piercing sound precedes a blinding, white-hot explosion that sends a mushroom-shaped column of fire, smoke, and debris into the air. The resulting smoke cloud dissipates to its fullest reach, eventually appearing to freeze in place on the blue canvas of the sky. Then, as if in reverse, the cloud is sucked back into itself as the facility changes from a solid structure to liquid to pure molten lava with a violent eruption, mushrooming once again into the sky. Frozen once again in the air for a few moments, the lava falls to the ground, along the way transforming into a heavy snowfall. All that is left of the facility and everything that was once there is a patch of ice.

The spaceship rockets out of the earth's atmosphere like a spinning bullet from the barrel of a gun. It continues its trajectory out of control, leaving a long vapor tail.

"Christina, do you see those yellow switches?"

She nods.

"Throw the first and the third--but not the second."

Her hand struggles to reach the switches. After throwing the first one her hand falls to her side. "I can't reach the next one, Joe."

"Christina, you have to concentrate. Our lives are in your hands."

Joe's words sink in loud and clear. She musters every bit of strength in her psyche. Taking deep, slow breaths, she focuses her entire being on moving her hand against the centrifugal force and toward the switches. The rolling and vibration of the ship causes the switch panel to appear as a blur. Every inch of her skin is covered with perspiration and every hair on her body is rigid. She continues commanding her hand to move toward the life-saving switch. Her trembling hand claws at the panel. She inches her hand along the sides of the panel, fearing if she lets go now it will all be over. Her energy is completely spent, and the only thing moving her hand forward is the adrenaline. Her long fingers climb onto the switch.

She is about to push the button when Joe notices something.

"NOT THE SECOND, THE THIRD."

Her fingers move away from the second switch and lock onto the third. Painfully bending her fingers around the switch, she manages to pull down the lever. A loud hissing sound is heard as they begin to stabilize. "Now what?" she implores.

"Look above you. You will see a series of switches labeled thrusters."

She looks up. She is dizzy and close to passing out.

"Christina... stay with me."

"I don't feel too good."

"Concentrate on the switches, Christina."

"Okay, Joe."

"Throw all the switches that say 'left side'."

Her other hand reaches for the switches, and she manages to throw them before passing out. The thrusters come on and the ship continues to stabilize. After twenty seconds it finally stops spinning.

With the ship stabilized and out of the earth's atmosphere, it heads directly toward the moon. Joe looks at Christina and feels for a pulse. "Good, you're still with us."

SIXTEEN

A group of men are gathered in a smoke-filled room. The windows are closed. An ornate mahogany table carved with occult images commands the center of the room. Heavy patterned material is draped above the windows. Rays of sunlight creep into the room through gaps in the curtains. Hand-crocheted doilies hold the heavy leaded baccarat glasses. Nazi flags hang on all four sides of the room. A large portrait of Adolf Hitler oversees the meeting from the head of the table. In front of each man is an oversized ashtray sporting a 7-inch Cohiba cigar along with a detailed report that will be the subject of the meeting. A phone sits in the center of the table.

The atmosphere is serious and sinister. By the looks of the room it is hard to imagine that World War II is over.

The men are in their fifties and sixties, with the exception of two that are much younger. Each man is dressed in a suit and tie and bearing a swastika on his left arm. Behold the cartel member elite. Heinrick, with a chiseled face, is known to openly wear a swastika on his lapel. Deswick, bald and officious, heads the cartel's space program. Klaus is an evil-looking man whose appearance is telling; he is capable of doing harm to just about anyone with extreme prejudice. Terrance and Adrian, both in their late twenties, are learning the cartel ropes while they prove themselves by doing the cartel's dirty work, namely murder. Heinrick addresses the group in a thick German accent.

"Gentlemen, I have called you all here today to relay some terrible news. The Pole facility has been destroyed."

The men in the room look at one another in disbelief. Klaus looks up from the report he is reading.

"How about Dr. Luctac?"

"No one could have survived the catastrophe."

Deswick is visibly upset.

"How could such a thing happen?"

Terrance and Adrian look at each other, anticipating another opportunity to prove their loyalty and worthiness to the cartel. Heinrick continues.

"We are not sure how this happened. However, our space station has been tracking one of our crafts that launched before the explosion. It appears the two people on board may be responsible for the deaths of our fellow members."

Deswick looks at the group, clears his throat.

"As head of our space division, I will leave for the station immediately." He looks at each member of the group, his eyes finally coming to rest on Terrance and Adrian. "You two will accompany me. I assure you this is where it will end."

Terrance and Adrian smile. "Is there a preferred method of termination?" asks Terrance.

Heinrick looks at them and then at the group. His expression becomes cold as ice, and he means what he says to the nth degree. "Terrance, Adrian, you have always been creative in your work."

There are sinister smiles from the members.

"Any suggestions on method of termination, gentlemen?" There is no response. Heinrick turns to his henchmen. "Adrian and Terrance specialize in... unique tortures and death sentences. I believe they may have a suggestion. Gentlemen, the floor is yours."

Adrian clears his throat. "Space can be a very cold place, especially if you are floating in it without any oxygen."

Terrance adds, "Of course, decompressing someone slowly in a bay also has its pluses. As the outside vacuum of space slowly sucks the air out of the chamber, the body swells until it bursts. It is extremely painful."

The members look at one another with apparent satisfaction. Heinrick appears content.

"Okay, it's settled. The three of you will leave right away. Deswick, I leave our future in your hands."

"Then the future is secure. Heil Hitler."

The group responds in kind.

A hologram at Switchblade operations illustrates the last moments of the explosion at the Pole facility, including the spacecraft launch. Surgeon is giving the details.

"It seems that a ship launched just before the explosion."

Agent Rachel, late twenties, is an Asian beauty with a computer for a brain. She is operations' answer to analysis.

"As you can see from this hologram, the ship was launched in a random panic pattern."

Soren looks at Rachel. "In layman's terms, please?"

"It means that, taking into account other data as well, I am convinced that Joe, Christina, Sal, and Luis may all be on that ship."

"Are you sure?"

"Right before the explosion we were receiving a message. It was terminated due to particle interference. The codes are Joe's. It is therefore logical to conclude that at the very least Joe is on board."

Vincent races into the room out of breath. "Sir, I have some more information."

"What is it?"

"Our field ops spotted Terrance and Adrian with an unidentified man in the Swiss Alps. Shortly after that our space station alerted us of another ground launch."

"Any heading on the launch?"

"Yes sir: the moon."

"Sounds like a regular tea party on the dark side of the moon. Anything else?"

Vincent smiles. "Yes, sir. The trail that led us to Terrance and Adrian uncovered the whereabouts of two key cartel members." Vincent points to the large monitor, which shows photographs of the two men. Surgeon steps closer to the monitor.

"Heinrick and Klaus! The cat and mouse game continues." He turns to Rachel. "You head one of the teams. I'll take the other. We are close to shutting down this group for good. These targets are to be erased at any cost. And I do mean any cost. Questions?" No one responds. "Good. That's all for now."

"Sir."

"Yes, Rachel."

"Wouldn't it be better to capture these men and try to find out who their leader is? I mean, we have never been this close before."

"I wish it was that easy. These men would kill themselves before giving up any information, especially the name of their leader. Just follow my orders."

She nods and leaves the room.

The cartel's space station is more advanced and more secretive than that of any government agency. The private funding raised to develop and build it enabled the cartel to acquire the best scientific minds of the century. The station, roughly half the size of Manhattan, is complete with monorails and flying transportation. The inhabitants live the lives of chosen ones in that they are void of the need for anything. At their disposal are the finest quality foods and the most diverting entertainments. The cartel's steady and undetected habitual drugs are the result of the station's happy inhabitants. It is the perfect society.

The control room is lined with glass, affording a view of space witnessed by few people. The constellations are rich in detail, with a never-ending sky highlighting a heavenly show of meteorites and their gaseous displays of beauty. In addition to the humans working on the station are androids and robots that are constantly on the move or flying around the room. It is a busy place.

An android walks over to the commander in charge. "Commander Androvich, we are tracking two ships heading towards the station."

"Who's on board?"

"The closer ship has not responded to our attempts at contact. The second ship is carrying Deswick and two passengers."

"Passengers? I know what that means." He turns to the communications officer. "Lt. Pelum, when the first ship is in range you will send a signal that resembles an automated computer docking signal. Then lock on the tractor beam and land it in Dock 7 Delta."

"Yes, sir. And the second ship?"

"The second ship is authorized to land on its own."

"Yes, sir."

Commander Androvich turns back to the android. "Have Chief Security Officer Rensher meet me in the briefing room."

"Right away, sir."

SEVENTEEN

A nondescript truck trundles quietly down an alley and pulls to one side. Whirring noises are heard, and a few thin antennas go up while stabilizers lower next to each wheel. The truck softly rocks while hydraulic adjustments are made to achieve a perfect balance.

Inside is Musky. He is in his mid-twenties and wears wire-rim glasses. He is the operations field tactical controller. Along with a few other men he is setting up command central. Computers are booted and earpieces go on. Musky gives last minute instructions to bring operations online. Three monitors show the positions of the team, which is ready to do its job.

"Rachel, this is Musky. Do you copy?"

"Copy. In place."

"Agent Soren?"

"In place."

"Agent Vincent?"

"Copy that."

"Our target should be here soon. Keep alert."

Musky turns to one of the men in the truck. "Could they have picked a busier street?"

Pedestrians and traffic fill the avenues as the snow falls. It is going to be a white Christmas in the city. Shoppers are in the holiday spirit. The street is lit by the soft glow of countless colorful Christmas decorations. A Santa talks to a little girl, who gleefully gives him her Christmas list. Lovers hold hands as the smell of roasting chestnuts wafts from the carts of street vendors and permeates the air. A man wearing a full-length cashmere overcoat exits a store holding a large bag filled with gifts. He stops, pulls off his leather gloves, reaches inside his coat, and pulls out a cigar and lights it.

Rachel observes the hustle and bustle of the festivities through a high-powered scope. She pans the street and stops at the man in the cashmere coat. It is Klaus.

"Listen up, team. I have visual on our target in front of Claus Christmas store."

Vincent responds, "Got him, but no shot."

"Contact," echoes Soren as he continues to search for an opening. A bus pulls into his field of view.

"NG. Got a bus in my way."

Musky makes the call. "Okay, Rachel, it's yours."

"I'm not clear yet."

Rachel is fully focused. She has him in her crosshairs, but people keep obscuring her view. Her finger moves to the safety and clicks it off.

"I'm live."

"Take the shot," Musky orders.

"Negative--civilians."

Rachel has Klaus periodically in her sites, but because of the obstacles she has an extremely narrow window of opportunity to shoot.

"Rachel, this may be our only chance. Take the shot."

Her finger tightens around the trigger. She has a clear shot at Klaus.

"I'm taking the shot."

Just as her finger tightens a bit more, a woman holding a baby steps in front of Klaus to ask him a question.

"Shit," says Rachel into the microphone.

"Talk to me, Rachel. Is there a problem?"

"My shot just evaporated."

Musky and the two other men listen intently to the developing situation. Musky is aware of what must happen and looks at his fellow operatives. They have all been trained to accept civilian casualties of war. Faced with the hardest decision of his life, he speaks slowly into the microphone.

"We can't wait any longer. This target is too important." There is no response from Rachel. "Rachel, do you hear me?" Still no answer. "Rachel, let me remind you Surgeon said 'at any cost'. Do you copy that?"

Rachel is sweating. Her finger quivers. She has the mother and child in her sights. She remembers the baby she lost that went full term and how painful that was for her. Could she take the life of a child and its mother for the sake of the mission? What cause can be so important that two innocent people have to die for its sake? As a professional she knows that one bullet will quickly end all three lives without pain. Rachel rests her head on the butt of her rifle with her finger firmly wrapped around the trigger. The growing noise of the street becomes a cacophony, including the sound of the bus leaving the stop.

Inside the truck, the three men look at one another uncertainly. Suddenly, a shot rings out. At street level, the mother is screaming as Klaus flies through a plate glass window. The mother and baby run for their lives. Panic has transformed the once happy street, which is now filled with shopping bags flying in all directions.

"This is Soren. The bus cleared and the target has been terminated."

A pilot and his co-pilot, both in their mid to late forties, are standing in an open hanger. The pilot is on a cell phone to Heinrick.

"We will arrive in ten minutes. Have the jet ready."

The pilot ends the call and turns to his co-pilot. "We're on in ten."

A man comes around the corner. He approaches the men, keeping to the shadows. The co-pilot nudges the pilot.

"This is a private hanger, sir. May I help you?"

The man says nothing and continues to approach. The pilot pulls out a revolver, but it is too late. A bullet hits him in the chest and he falls to the ground. The co-pilot turns to run. His body flies backwards with a single bullet to the forehead, landing next to the dead pilot. One of Surgeon's agents is standing next to the dead man. He is dressed in a co-pilot's uniform. The man in the shadows joins him. It is Surgeon, dressed as a pilot.

"You heard the man. We have ten minutes to get the jet ready. I'll call it in."

Surgeon takes out his cell phone and dials. The phone has the distinct sound of a scrambled line. Surgeon waits patiently for the phone to be answered. "Base, all is well."

"Are you in control of the bird?"

"Affirmative. We will rendezvous at drop point." He hangs up the phone and looks around. Satisfied that the operation is going according to plan, he turns and climbs into the jet.

The engines are just warming up as a limousine pulls alongside the waiting jet. The car door opens and Heinrick climbs out. He boards the jet, the door closes, and the plane immediately taxis onto the runway. A full moon lights the way of the jet as it takes off.

A stunning flight attendant in her mid-twenties walks up to Heinrick, who is reading a newspaper.

"May I get you something to drink, sir?"

Heinrick looks up and is immediately aroused by her beauty. "Are you new, my dear?"

"Actually, this is my first day."

"Do you know who I am?"

It is clear she is uncomfortable with his question. "Yes, sir. I was told to take very good care of you and make sure you get anything you wish."

He smiles at the misdirected thought. "Please, sit down."

She hesitates, but when he motions to the seat across from him, she sits. He gets up and sits next to her, and immediately he begins trying to undress her. She jumps up.

"Excuse me, sir, but I am a professional flight attendant."

Heinrick stands up. "You are what I say you are."

"I don't think so."

Before she can say another word, Heinrick smashes her in the face. She falls to the floor. He gets on top of her and looks her over. "As I said, you are what I say you are, and right now you are an object for my pleasure." Heinrick tears open her blouse and begins to undo her bra roughly. She screams.

"Scream all you like, my dear. My pilot and co-pilot will not save you, and as for me... I like the sounds of screaming."

She struggles to free herself, but his strength is too much for her. He slaps her again, splitting open her lower lip. She begins to grow weaker. Heinrick looks at her and sees the blood on her lip. He wipes it and licks his bloodstained finger as he smiles at her sadistically. It begins to dawn on her that she is his helpless prey and there is nothing she can do about it. Proud of his pending conquest, he begins groping her breasts. She is crying and pleading.

"Please, don't do this. STOP IT, YOU BASTARD."

She continues to struggle to no avail. Heinrick punches her once again, splitting her lip again.

"Don't ever call me a bastard, you piece of shit bitch." Heinrick begins to rip off more clothing when a foot lands squarely in his face. He falls on his back and looks up to see who kicked him.

"Surgeon."

Surgeon is standing over him with a silencer attached to his handgun. Looking at the scared flight attendant, Surgeon says, "Get up and sit over there." He turns to Heinrick. "And you sit over here." The distraught flight attendant gets up, covers herself, and takes a seat. Surgeon looks at her, then at his agent.

"Check the gear."

The agent goes to check the gear. Surgeon sits across from Heinrick, who stares at him.

"You know, Surgeon, together we could have a very lucrative arrangement."

"By that you mean senselessly killing people and destroying lives?"

"Surgeon, you are a smart man. Look at your government, or for that matter, any government. Do you really think anything has changed since the beginning of time?"

"For people like you, nothing changes except the faces of those you kill."

Heinrick smiles at the thought. "You're idealistic. The players in the game control you while you are still sitting outside. You have keys to the game, but you don't even realize it. I could show you how the game is played."

"You are one sick bastard. You sit there talking to me about the game. You and your cartel members trade lives, countries, drugs, weapons, and political favors like most people change underwear."

"You amaze me. You go out on death missions for your government, but have you ever once looked into the eyes of the person whose life you have ended? Have you ever considered the pain you bring to their friends and loved ones? You are a salaried hypocrite. You probably go to church with your family on Sunday, then the next day you are perched with your team on a roof waiting to take out a target. Your feelings about death are the same as mine. Life is meaningless unless you have power. Life ends soon enough, so if you happen to end a few lives prematurely, so what? In the grand scheme of things, it is insignificant."

"The targets we take out deserve their fate."

"How do you know that? Because your government told you? Are you that naive?"

"What is it with you guys? Why do you feel the need to control everything? Tell me."

"It is simple. People are like sheep. If you give them enough to get by, they are content. Most of them are unmotivated and lazy. It is their laziness that makes them vulnerable. Their vulnerability makes them dangerous because they eventually want more without having to do anything for it. Can you guess what happens? They become unmanageable and revolt. They become unruly."

Surgeon cannot resist interjecting some sarcasm. "Essentially you really are a humanitarian?"

Heinrick laughs out loud. "Humanitarian? No, I don't think so. We see people as a commodity. If you have enough of the commodity, then you have a strong workforce. Fear of physical and mental terror is a proven and reliable means of control. When they come into alignment with our rules they actually are fulfilled. They become the sheep they started out as. Everyone wins."

"You know, Heinrick, before this talk I thought you were just sick. Now I'm beginning to see the light."

"Then perhaps we can come to some equitable arrangement?"

Surgeon's agent comes out of the cockpit.

"Everything is set."

The flight attendant and agent exchange glances as they see Heinrick and Surgeon staring at each other.

"Sir, everything is set."

"Surgeon, I think it is time we explain to your agent friend what is going on here."

The agent is confused. "Surgeon, what the hell is he talking about?"

Heinrick is smiling as he lights a cigarette.

Surgeon explains to the agent, "It's all about the game."

"Sir?"

"You see, Surgeon, even those on the inside don't know they are pawns in the game."

Surgeon is deep in thought, then he gets up, grabs Heinrick, and pulls him out of his seat as Heinrick's cigarette goes flying.

"Get up, you piece of shit. You want to play games? Well, I have a game for you. It's called chicken."

The agent and Surgeon drag Heinrick kicking and screaming to the cockpit. Heinrick is put into the pilot's seat and handcuffed so he has no access to the controls.

"What are you doing, Surgeon?"

"Can you fly a plane, Heinrick?"

"No."

"Good."

Surgeon and the agent make some control adjustments and switch on the autopilot with a new heading.

"Surgeon, you are making a huge mistake. Even if you kill me we will win. There is no avoiding it. We have been planning this for over 60 years. You are nothing in the game. Do you hear me? Nothing."

Surgeon turns to his agent. "Get you and the flight attendant ready."

"You have 30 seconds, sir."

"Go. I'll be right there." The agent leaves the cockpit.

Surgeon feels a responsibility to the mission. "Heinrick, I'll give you one chance, which is more than you ever gave anyone. Name the head of your cartel and I will free you."

He sighs. "Either way it becomes a death warrant. If I tell you, I will be dead before the night is over. We are too strong and too many. My friend, you must understand that your request is unreasonable. However, I can make you one of the richest men alive without anyone knowing about it."

"You know, Heinrick, money never really mattered much to me." He gets nose to nose. "I guess

I will say goodbye." Surgeon begins to leave the cockpit.

"You won't leave me here. You are bluffing. Your superiors will want me alive. Surgeon, are you listening?" As he pleads, he notices in the distance a mountain in the direct flight path of the plane. He begins to struggle.

Surgeon is strapping on a parachute. The flight attendant is panicking.

"No fucking way am I putting a parachute on my back."

Surgeon toys with her. "You're right. We only have two."

She realizes the direness of the situation. "What are you saying? You're going to leave me?"

"Well, since you don't want to wear a parachute, I assume you want to stay with your boss."

"My boss? That asshole? I only met him tonight." Surgeon and the agent go to the door and begin to release it. "Hey, wait a minute. If you open that door, I'll get swept out."

They continue what they're doing.

"Okay, have it your way. Give me a chute."

"He isn't kidding. There are only two chutes," says the agent.

"Oh, my God, I'm going to die... Shit... I can't believe this... No way... Shit... I've never been married, or had kids.... Hey, what kind of animals would leave a wom--"

Surgeon cuts her off with a blow to the jaw. He picks her up and ties her body to his with a rope. He looks at the agent. "I didn't want to listen to that all the way down. Kick the door."

The agent opens the door, and the three jump out of the plane. Two parachutes open as the jet continues on its bearing.

From Heinrick's point of view a towering mountain is fast approaching. His face fills with terror as he realizes this is the end. Just before the impact he lets out a blood-curdling scream. The plane smashes into the side of the mountain, exploding on impact and instantaneously cutting short Heinrick's scream. The fiery ball can be seen for miles. A dark destructive voice has been silenced forever.

EIGHTEEN

Space is a still and peaceful place, with a depthless view of stars and swirling colorful galaxies that quiz the limits of the human imagination. Joe looks thoughtfully from space to Christina's face. He moves his eyes from her long hair to her eyebrows, wishing so much that it were his lips tracing the features of her face. His fantasy continues, going from her sleeping eyes, down her nose, to her full lips. Even after what they both have been through, her beauty still shines through. Her eyelids quiver then open wide, and her mouth gasps for air as she is jolted awake from a nightmare. Joe quickly looks away, adjusting some control knobs. After a moment he turns to her.

"Good morning."

"Where's the coffee?" she asks, stretching and eking out a delicate yawn.

He hands her a shirt. "Here, I found this. Yours is torn."

"Torn? Let me remind you I was shot."

"It's a scratch."

Christina is about to say something when a beeping sound comes from the console. She looks at Joe.

"We are being paged again."

She looks at him suspiciously, "How do you know that's what it is?"

He gives no response.

"Are you going to answer me?"

He reaches over and pushes a button. A face appears on a small monitor. It is the space station commander.

"This is Commander Androvich. Your ship is now on auto-command for docking. You will be docking in Bay 7 Delta."

The screen on the monitor goes black.

"He seems friendly enough," Christina says sarcastically.

"Androvich is as ruthless as they come," replies Joe without hesitation.

"You know this guy?"

He gets up. "I have a few things to take care of before we dock. Don't touch any of the controls, okay?"

"Like I would even know what I'm doing." Christina takes her portable communication device out from her belt and begins to contact Surgeon.

Joe grabs the device and smashes it. "Are you completely out of your mind? The second you link with base, we are dead. And that is assuming we aren't dead already."

Christina looks at him with suspicion. "Or is it you don't want base to know where we are?"

Joe shakes his head as he walks away. "We will land in about seven minutes."

A spacecraft lands inside the docking port. Its engines shut down and the door opens. Commander Androvich waits with Chief Security Officer Rensher along with several armed men. Once the door is open Deswick, Terrance, and Adrian step out. Deswick acknowledges his guests.

"Commander Androvich, Chief Rensher, you remember Terrance and Adrian." Greetings are exchanged.

"Deswick, there is a ship approaching the station under our tracking beam. They will be docking in 7 Delta in about three minutes."

"Excellent. Shall we go meet them?"

Rensher steps forward. "Are they the ones responsible for the Pole incident?"

"If they are, we will know soon enough."

Terrance and Adrian smile sadistically. Rensher turns to his android assistant. "Have an additional security team meet us in 7 Delta. No, wait a minute... On second thought, I want them to feel as though there is nothing wrong. When people are comfortable, they tend to make mistakes. Have the normal security precautions in place. Greet them as guests. After all, where can they go?"

The ship is silently guided toward a docking door. Joe and Christina are amazed at the size of the station. Joe types on the command keyboard.

"I thought you said not to touch the controls?"

Joe is concentrating and working very fast. The spacecraft approaches the final docking position and the landing gear touches down. Rensher, Androvich, and the android greet Joe and Christina. Deswick, Terrance, and Adrian are high above observing the docking area from behind large glass windows. The ship's door opens, and Joe and Christina step out.

"Welcome. I'm Commander Androvich, and this is Chief Security Officer Rensher."

"This is Christina, and my name is Joe."

Rensher wants to tear into the both of them like a pit bull, but he musters his self-control.

"You have had a long trip. Our android will escort you to your rooms, where you will refresh yourselves before joining the head of the station, Mr. Deswick, for dinner."

Christina looks down at herself. "You wouldn't happen to have any women's clothing around here, would you?"

The android steps forward. "As a matter of fact, we have one of the finest selections on Earth. I will be glad to take you to the clothing center."

"Yes. Thank you."

"Then it is settled. Enjoy your stay."

As the android leads Joe and Christina out of the docking bay Androvich looks up at Deswick, who nods his head.

NINETEEN

CMN news reporter Marilyn Rush is standing in front of NASA with Dr. Panopolous. There is a news buzz in the air, the likes of which hasn't been seen since the Kennedy assassination. She is a bit hyper, to say the least. She addresses the camera.

"We are here live in front of NASA, where scientists are trying to understand what happened at the North Pole and what effect it could have on our planet. I have here with me the head of the space program, Dr. Panopolous, whose team is responsible for polar monitoring from space. Doctor, what can you tell us about the anomaly that recently occurred at the North Pole, and is it a threat to life on this planet?"

Dr. Panopolous clears his throat. "Well, so far what we have learned is that the pole had a spontaneous meltdown--"

Marilyn anxiously interrupts him. "A meltdown? Does that mean we should expect tidal waves, the size of which mankind has never seen? Are we doomed, doctor?"

The doctor looks at her confused. "As I was saying, the pole had a meltdown and then reconstituted itself immediately. It is a phenomenon the scientific community finds baffling, but--"

She interrupts again. "If the scientific community is baffled, then it seems hopeless for us all. Will this cause a global warming or cooling trend that could end life on our planet, doctor?"

The doctor shakes his head and turns to her. "A little too much coffee this morning, miss?" He then turns to the news camera. "We are studying the effects of this situation. Currently it is stable and probably poses no threat to life on earth. We are very lucky it reformed as fast as it did. Otherwise it could have had a significant impact on the biological fate of our planet."

She steps away from the doctor and addresses the camera. "There you have it, ladies and gentlemen. NASA is unsure of what has happened at the Pole, and there is serious concern for life as we know it. But please, stay calm and do not panic. Our government has the situation well under control." The live broadcast from NASA wraps up as the reporter signs off.

"We will keep you up to date on this exclusive news story that could affect life on this planet. I'm Marilyn Rush for CMN. Now back to the studio for continued coverage."

The screen goes black. Surgeon and the two teams are in the room watching the news broadcast. Surgeon is smiling. "Now that is what I call brilliant reporting."

A series of alerts activate several of their systems. Rachel turns to an agent.

"Start tracking the signal and begin download procedures."

"Right." The agent begins typing on a keyboard while other agents busy themselves at their stations.

Surgeon takes control. "Anything, anyone?"

The sounds of keyboards being hammered along with various, "Negative here" echo throughout the room.

Agent #1 blurts out, "Got something, but it's scrambled."

"Can you unscramble the message?"

"Working on it."

"I got another section coming in scrambled," says Agent #2.

Rachel works fiendishly at her station. "Confirmed. There are five scrambled and coded signals coming in." She calls out to the group, "Start a decoding sequence. Stack dump into bins 9 Alpha, 2 Charlie, 3 Baker, 7 Gamma, 6 Zed."

Monitors show endless strings of coded symbols, figures, and blueprint diagrams. On the large screen at the front of the room, all the stations have their individual monitors showing what they are receiving, while the large monitor shows the figures and symbols beginning to merge into a singular un-coded message.

Surgeon watches as things progress. He takes a key from around his neck and goes over to a safe. Everyone in the room takes notice as Surgeon pushes the key into the lock and turns it. The safe opens, and he withdraws a large book stamped with "TOP SECRET" in red letters on the cover. Surgeon goes over to his desk and opens the book. He looks at the incoming message and then at the book. The typing in the room has stopped, and he finally notices all is quiet. He looks up and sees everyone staring at him.

"As soon as I know what is going on you all will be the first to know. Now, please continue your work so we don't lose any information."

Everyone resumes working. Surgeon is deep in thought as he studies the book to the sound of fingers feverishly entering data into the computers.

Christina is in a bra and panties. Scattered all over the dressing area is the vast assortment of clothing she has been trying on. She is busily stashing various objects on her body. She snaps something behind the front clip on her bra, opens a lighter, makes an adjustment, and looks inside her shoe. She smiles.

"Okay, now I am ready for dinner." She looks in the mirror. "Well... almost ready.

The dining room is cozy and rivals that of any five-star restaurant. A grand mantel warms the room, which fills with the smell of burning one hundred-year-old sycamore pine. From the looks of this place you would never guess you were in orbit behind a moon in outer space. The smell from the kitchen is positively mouth-watering. The wafting aroma of venison is mixed with the smell of sauté spinach in wine, butter, and garlic. The wine has been carefully selected to accent the taste of the venison. A Château Latour has been decanted and sits waiting patiently to be enjoyed. The long stem candles have been lit, imparting to the room a gentle amber glow.

Deswick is standing by the fireplace savoring a before-dinner glass of Taylor 1963 port when the automatic door opens. The light and activity in the corridor serve as a harsh reminder that this inviting atmosphere is part of an orbiting station. Its cold metallic appearance provides a harsh counterpoint to the warm environment of the dining room. A silhouetted figure enters the room. It is Joe. The door shuts behind him, the mood quickly reestablished. He looks around, taking in the room's immaculate details.

"Very impressive."

"Thank you. My name is Colonel Deswick. Where is your... Wife? Partner?"

"Colleague. She should be..."

The door opens again and then closes immediately. Both men turn to see Christina. She is wearing a magnificent dress that accents every curve on her flawless body. She sashays across the room directly over to Deswick. Joe watches while his heart threatens to skip a beat. He thought he had seen her at her best, but this is beyond anything he knows. She is angelic.

"Hello, my name is Christina."

Deswick kisses her hand. "Enchanté. Colonel Deswick at your service. Are you hungry?"

"Oui, j'ai faim."

"Ah, parlez vous Francais?"

"Oui, un peu."

Joe is feeling left out. "What's for dinner? It smells delicious."

"Venison. I shot it myself."

Joe and Christina exchange glances.

Deswick continues. "Shall we sit?"

While the three of them enjoy their dinner, Surgeon has finished reading his codes and looks up from the book. His eyes are wide.

"Oh, shit."

All heads in the room turn toward him. Then everyone looks to Rachel.

"What is it, sir?" she asks.

"The message we intercepted is coded to change the positions of all the laser defense satellites."

One agent dares to say what is on everyone's mind. "Uh, what exactly does that mean, sir?"

Surgeon takes a deep breath and finishes. "In less than two hours, the satellites will reposition themselves at an angle to the sun which will create a reflective heat targeted directly at our space station." Rachel now grasps the implications. "Once it begins, it will heat the station to approximately 7,000 degrees Fahrenheit, causing it to explode."

As Rachel is explaining things to the group, several strategically positioned satellites come alive with blinking lights and sequential beeps. One by one they begin to change their positions. The first one begins to open. The next one follows suit, and the next. They all open in perfect synchronicity with reflector dishes rising from the center. The dishes fan apart and expand outwards. Each dish is approximately a quarter of a mile in diameter. In the middle of each dish is a laser apparatus. One by one the lasers begin to glow and take on life. The pulsations serve as a preamble to what will ensue: total destruction.

In a foreboding and unpredictable coincidence, the candles on the dining room table have burned down to stubs, dripping wax on the starched tablecloth. The meal and desert entailed a perfect gastronomic experience. While Joe and Christina sip their cognac, Deswick lights a Cuban cigar. He is the quintessential host. After a few satisfying puffs, Deswick makes a toast.

"To all our comrades with a singular purpose--to rule the world."

Much to their chagrin, Joe and Christina join in on the loathsome toast. The three clink glasses. The final dishes are cleared from the table as Deswick escorts his guests to oversized lounging chairs arranged by the fire. They all settle in and relax. Deswick senses his guests are vulnerable enough for him to proceed.

"Now, shall we talk?"

Christina coyly says, "Isn't that what we have been doing?"

"You are very beautiful, my dear, but don't insult my intelligence."

Christina quiets down.

Joe distracts Deswick from Christina. "What's on your mind?"

"Congratulations. You managed to escape the Polar disaster. And now I ask a very simple question: Who are you really?"

"We are comrades."

Deswick regards them with a serious expression and a tone to match.

"Are we going to play games, Joe? You two are very skilled agents. We can use people like you. Or you can just die here on the station and never be heard from again." Deswick turns to Christina. "N'est ce pas?"

Christina feels trapped. "What do you want?"

"Direct. I like that. Our group needs people in the field to implement our ideals."

"Ideals? Is that what you call annihilation?"

"Look at it this way. Life is very short and you should live with the fruits that are available. When we die, there is no one here to judge our actions, nor will anyone care. It is an old government trick to make the people believe there is such a thing as morality. People like you and I realize the truth of life. The only difference is I play the game and you are played by the game."

"You may be right, but I'd rather be played by it than kill innocent people."

"There are no innocent people, Christina."

Joe's watch begins vibrating as a low light comes on. He subtly glances down. The clock face reads: Less than 2 hours.

Deswick presses his point. "You didn't think about that when you destroyed the Pole facility."

Joe and Christina look at each other.

Joe calmly looks up and engages Deswick. "Those weren't innocent people."

"My point exactly. No innocent people. They knew what they were doing and still did it. Why? Because they never expected to pay the price. Instead, they wanted a piece of the New World and the power that comes with being on the winning side. Don't be fools. Join the new order and take a place in history." He plays for Christina's vanity. "You could stay young and beautiful for eternity with our cloning program."

"And I suppose you will also waive all my parking fines?"

Deswick stares at her with death daggers in his eyes. He pushes a button, and Adrian and Terrance come into the room.

"Joe, you are intelligent. What will your decision be?"

"You have my attention, but what assurances do I have?"

Christina cannot believe her ears. She has finally heard enough.

"You bastard... How could you?"

"Look who's talking. You used every means at your disposal to bring me into your idealistic group."

Terrance looks on and says mockingly, "How touching." Turning to Deswick, he adds, "Can I kill her now?"

Adrian becomes equally melodramatic. "You selfish brute. What about me? Who do I kill?"

Deswick laughs ruthlessly at the cruel banter. "You see, Christina, they're fighting over you." His smile subsides. "Terrance, Adrian, take them both. Have our hero here kill the girl. If he does, then he is with us. If not, nothing lost. I'll inform Widow. Nothing like a good torture session to round out the day."

The clock on the satellite reads 1 hour 45 minutes. The satellites continue to rotate toward the sun. The laser arms pulsate, gathering the sun's energy. Inside NASA's control room is bedlam. People are running all over the place. The watch commander is perplexed at his readouts. He turns to one of the attendants.

"What the hell is going on here?"

"I don't know, sir. None of the satellites are responding. They are going into laser formation mode."

"What's the target?"

"If I'm reading this right, there is no target or threat so far."

"Explain."

"The target is the other side of the moon. There is nothing of value there. Not even a remote satellite to knock out."

"Make sure we aren't being overridden by our enemies. What could those bastards be up to?

"Sir, the override signal is coming from a code clearance I've never even heard of."

"Is it friendly?"

"No way to know, sir."

"That's not good enough." He turns to his personal assistant, Lana Andrews, who is the epitome of military efficiency.

Before he can utter a word, she says, "Sir, should I call the Joint Chiefs?"

"How is it that you always know what I am thinking?"

"You taught me well, sir. How about the President?"

Succumbing to her flattery, he says, "Not yet. Let's see how this plays out for a while."

Inside the space station's decompression room several androids operate computers. The androids are, in fact, built right into the console from the waist up. They have the ability to turn 360 degrees but are permanently attached to their station. A door opens, and Joe, Christina, Terrance, and Adrian enter. Terrance and Adrian are carrying large space-age weapons. They walk over to a circular chamber sitting in the middle of the expansive room. Adrian pushes a button and a door spins opens.

"Well, love, here is where you meet your maker."

Terrance continues, "You see, we put you in there and close the door."

Then Adrian, as if reading a script, adds, "We push this button here." He points to a button.

Terrance continues, "The oxygen is slowly released into outer space."

Back to Adrian: "The room reaches zero oxygen."

Terrance illustrates her grisly fate with exaggerated gestures. "Your body implodes."

"Makes a hell of a mess," adds Adrian.

"But it is foolproof," says Terrance with a smile.

Adrian concludes, "Well, Terrance, I think our contestant has run out of time."

"Adrian, you may do the honors.

"No, remember what Deswick said." He turns his attention to Joe. "It's all yours, my friend."

Joe feels trapped. He takes one step toward Christina.

Christina thinks quickly. "Excuse me. Don't I get a final request?"

Adrian and Terrance look at each other.

"Terrance, I hope it's not a cigarette."

"You are so right because smoking is bad for your health." The two laugh uncontrollably at their sophomoric humor.

"Actually, I was thinking that if I have to die, I would really like to have sex one last time before I go. And I want you." She points at Terrance. Joe looks at her and then Terrance.

"Me?"

"Yes. And I want you two to watch."

"Can you handle that, Terrance?"

Terrance eagerly sets down his weapon. "I'm game." He goes over and starts to kiss her awkwardly. He is a bit rough at first. Christina stops him and looks him in the eye.

"Terrance, I'm not going to fight you. You will have me completely. But let's be gentle, okay."

"Sure."

"Good. Now unbutton my blouse and take it off."

He does so. "That is much better, isn't it?"

Staring at her breasts, he says, "It is too bad you have to die. You have great looking..." He looks up at her. "Eyes."

In a very seductive voice with body language to match, she says, "I want you to come real close to my body and unsnap my bra. The snap is in the front."

Terrance becomes paranoid. "Why close?"

"When they come out, I want to feel your warm face against my skin as you kiss them."

Terrance is like a kid in a candy store, smiling from ear to ear. He looks at Adrian, who is also focused on the unveiling. His hands reach the front clasp, and his quivering fingers curl around the snap and begin to undo it. He lowers his head to her breasts as his hands continue their work. Without warning, a mist shoots from her bra. He pulls away screaming and clawing at his eyes.

"My eyes... My fucking eyes are on fire."

Joe responds quickly, knocking Adrian down as Christina kicks Terrance in the groin. Terrance grabs his groin, then his eyes, then his groin again, not knowing which hurts more. Confused and off balance, he stumbles into the decompression chamber. Christina quickly closes the door on him. As Terrance's eyes begin to clear, he realizes where he is and begins clawing at the window in the chamber. His eyes are blood red.

Joe shakes his head. "Nifty bra, Christina."

Adrian sees an opportunity and kicks the weapon out of Joe's hand. They begin to fight, exchanging blows and kicks. The two men are evenly matched. As the fight draws out, Christina sees Terrance's weapon and reaches for it. A foot steps on the weapon, preventing her from grabbing it. Christina looks up. A weapon held by a pair of gloved hands is aimed between Christina's eyes. It is the Widow. Eventually, Joe overpowers Adrian and is prepared to kill him.

"Hold on, man. Don't shoot. I'll make you a deal."

"Such as?"

"I know things."

"The only thing I want to know from you is that you're dead. Say goodbye, asshole.

Joe is about to pull the trigger when he hears a voice.

"Drop the weapon or I splatter this beauty's brains all over you."

Looking over his shoulder, he sees Christina's predicament. Widow's face is still obscured, hidden in shadow. Joe slowly drops his gun.

Widow instructs Christina, "Put your clothes back on."

Adrian looks over and is terrified to see who his savior is. "Widow, Terrance is in the decompression chamber."

"I know. I despise failure." The gloved hand reaches over and pushes the button. Terrance lets out a scream.

"NOOOOOOO. PLEASE STOP," pleads Terrance to no avail.

Just as the words leave his mouth his body caves in then explodes, blood and tissue saturating the window. Joe and Adrian stand up. Widow steps out from the shadows. Her face is visible for the first time. Joe looks at her in astonishment.

"You? I don't understand."

"Hello, Joe."

"You are Widow?"

"Yes, Joe."

"But you and Dad... Mother, how could you..."

"I'm not your mother, you pathetic man," she snaps.

"What about the grave and the locket?"

"We simply switched the gravestone to make you think your mother was still alive. The locket is in fact your mother's, but it was my idea to have Mommy give her lost son a tear-jerking moment... a moment of weakness. We knew you would want to carry out your parents' mission. Did you like the note I sent to you about Christina? Don't trust her, Love, Mom? You and your kind are so easy to confuse. We know who you really are, Joe. Does she?"

Christina is confused. "What is she saying, Joe?"

"You mean you don't know, my dear?"

"Know what?"

"And you thought you were recruiting him."

"We did recruit him. So what?"

Behind his back Joe is twisting his watch. He knows that everything is on the line now. At this point he has nothing to lose. His heart breaks knowing that his parents truly are gone forever and that his lost past has been wrenched from his grasp for a second time. His sadness quickly turns to anger that fuels him to push through his feelings and accomplish what he came there for. There will be no prisoners, and anyone who gets in the way will be toast.

"Things are not what they appear to be. You see, my dear, your lover here is..."

Joe activates his watch and a blinding light flashes. He grabs Adrian and pulls him in front of himself, using him as a human shield as Widow opens fire. She hits Adrian, who begins to scream as the laser beam begins to liquefy his body, which leaks blood from every orifice until little is left of him but a puddle of tissue. Christina shoves Widow and breaks for the exit alongside Joe. As Widow prepares to fire her weapon Joe returns fire with Adrian's weapon. Widow pushes an alarm. The room immediately goes dark, with flashing red lights. A computer voice can be heard.

"Intruder alert. Security to Deck 23 Sector 5."

Joe and Christina hide behind stacked containers.

Christina stares at him. "What was all that about not knowing who you really are?"

"I hardly think this is the time to explain." Joe looks at his watch. "We have about ten minutes to get off this station and far, far away before we become part of this barbecue."

Armed men storm the area. There is an exchange of fire and bodies begin falling all over the place. Joe looks at his weapon. Christina can read his expression.

"Let me guess... You're almost out of whatever it is that thing uses for ammo."

"Give that girl a prize. See that opening in the wall? It leads to the flight deck. On three."

"Joe, before we go, would you really have killed me?"

He looks at her and kisses her. "I'm not sure." He makes a run for the opening.

Stunned, she says, "Not sure? What kind of answer is that?"

A laser explodes close to her head, jolting her back to her senses, and she runs for the opening. Widow sees Christina, aims, and fires. She is hit in the arm and falls. Joe hears her scream. He sees Widow and shoots back. He misses.

Widow runs out of the room screaming, "I'll make sure your death is a very painful one."

Joe goes over to Christina. "Nice run."

"Good thing the bitch has a lousy aim."

They get up. Christina sees a dead soldier and grabs his weapon. She stands up and angrily mows down several soldiers. Joe turns around and pulls her down.

"I hate to break up your score card, but we are about to be incinerated."

Christina looks at him. "Let me guess, you will explain that later, too."

"Exactly. Now can we go?"

Christina points the gun at Joe. He freezes. "You mean you would have killed me, huh?"

"Christina, I never said I would... What I was going..."

Their eyes lock. She fires the weapon. The shot passes over Joe's shoulder and hits a soldier who was sneaking up on him. The man falls dead at Joe's feet.

Christina blows at the end of the barrel cowgirl style. "You were saying?"

"Nice shot. Now, can we go?" Christina pulls out a lighter. Joe continues. "I don't think this is a good time for a smoke."

She flicks open the lighter and tosses it into the center of the room as she begins to run. "One... two... three... run for it!"

A sulfur-type explosion causes disorientation in the remaining soldiers. As they run full force, Joe smiles at Christina.

"Did you go to James Bond summer camp? Bra, lighter... I suppose the next surprise will come out of your shoe?"

In a serious voice, she says, "Let's hope we won't need to find out."

All the satellites have come to rest in their final position and are aimed at the space station. The satellite timers read 2 minutes. Each satellite is fully charged and pulsing. Rays are beginning to converge on the space station, forming a triangular vortex. Joe and Christina have taken the battle to engineering.

They scramble to reach the spacecraft so they can get off the station before it's too late. Laser fire ricochets all around them. The room is beginning to glow from the satellite laser beams, which are charging to full power.

"We are running out of time. It's now or never, Christina."

With lasers dicing the airspace around them, she is only able to catch glimpses of the room's layout. "Which way do we go?"

"I'm not sure, but I think it's this way."

As they make their way through engineering, the laser fire is relentless. Bodies are flying everywhere. Christina is knocking off soldiers like a carnival duck shoot while Joe tries to get the door to open.

"What's the holdup?"

"The damn computer must have overridden the controls."

Christina pushes Joe aside and blasts the panel. The door opens. "After you."

Joe goes through the door followed by Christina. Once through, the door slams shut behind them. They slowly turn around and see spacesuits and booster boots hanging from the walls. There is no other way out. They have managed to trap themselves inside a closet.

"Nice going."

Joe looks around trying desperately to find a way out. "Okay, we have an opportunity here."

Christina, exhausted and wounded, is losing her patience. "Opportunity? Are you completely out of your mind? Let me see if I have this right. An army of armed soldiers is pursuing us. You lead us into a closet with no way out, And now we have AN OPPORTUNITY?"

She collapses on the floor, exhausted. Joe goes and sits next to her.

"It will be all right."

At that she comes completely unglued. "ALL RIGHT? ALL RIGHT? WE ARE GOING TO DIE IN THIS ROOM AND YOU SAY IT'LL BE ALL RIGHT!"

"Rough day at the office, huh?"

She looks at him, utterly spent. They stare at each other for a moment. Then they both start to laugh. Joe looks around and sees the space booster boots. He gets up and checks the suits.

"Find something interesting, Joe, or are you just window shopping?"

"I have an idea."

She shakes her head and mutters, "We're saved."

Widow is with Deswick reviewing the station's situation. A computer voice comes on again. "The station's outer hull is reaching critical heat levels. A breech is imminent."

"Deswick, shut that off. We don't want to panic everyone."

"Widow, you need to leave the station now. I will make sure those two don't get out of here alive."

"You are a loyal man. Meet me in our Washington office when you have finished here." She leaves the room. His face portrays pure determination.

Joe and Christina have put on spacesuits.

"Now remember, when I blow the hole in the side of this wall we will be sucked into space. You will have to use your jet pack and boot boosters to stabilize. Then we have to fly to the upper level and make it to the docking area. They won't be expecting us to enter that way so we will have the element of surprise. Ready?"

"No."

"Right."

He fires at the wall, opening up a jagged hole in the side of the station that sucks all the oxygen out of the room. Joe and Christina come rocketing out encapsulated in the vacuum.

"Wowwwwwww... Shit."

"We're going to die, Joe."

"Hit the boosters. NOW!" They activate the backpack jets and booster boots. They begin to stabilize.

Inside NASA's control room the commotion remains at full tilt. The Joint Chiefs of Staff and other officials are gathered in the room listening to the watch commander.

"Gentlemen, we have determined that there is activity on the other side of the moon. It could be an invasion from space or one of our enemies launching an attack."

General Bedard has been warning the government for years about the possibility of just such a scenario. Inside he derides his commanders for not listening to him. His only hope is that they will take a lesson from the experience. Perhaps this will earn him another cluster for his collar. He knows he is right, and now he will show them his professional side by asking questions that no one has answers for.

"If it is an invasion from space, we are not equipped to deal with this... as I have been saying for the past ten years. If it is one of our enemies, it begs the question, what kind of launch are they capable of doing from the moon and how did they get it there in the first place?"

"Good questions, general."

"Then let's have some good answers.

"We have already gone to full alert, and all possible options have been analyzed and are already underway. Including something..." He hesitates.

"Well, let's say that we..."

"Cut the bullshit, commander," says Bedard. "Do you have something in development we don't know about, and if so, what the hell are the capabilities?"

As the general says these words out loud his insides begin to twist. Might they have actually taken him seriously after all and developed something without his knowledge? And if so then what could it be, and why was he excluded from what was essentially his vision? The attention of everyone in the room is on the watch commander.

"Perhaps we should go into the conference room for a briefing."

While the meeting has adjourned and reconvened in the conference room, a car slows to a stop on a side street near the Pentagon. A man gets out and plugs the meter. Securely tucked under his arm is an envelope. It is the one that Widow gave to him.

With a sense of determination and purpose he walks up the steps and into the Pentagon. He presents his identification to the guard and is cleared to enter. He walks down a long hallway and stops in front of the War Department Headquarters main entrance. Again he is cleared to enter. The envelope, which he now holds in his hands, bears an official government seal. The guard opens the door, and he enters the high security area, continuing along the designated path to another door, which is labeled Clearance Level 9 Only.

The man's clearance badge is checked, and he is permitted to enter the room. He walks directly to a desk and stops. He drops the envelope in the middle of the desk.

"Here are your new orders."

A pair of hands reaches for the envelope, which lift it up and begin to open it. Quickly the seated man reads his orders and puts down the envelope next to a nameplate on the desk. The plate reads: Jimmy Peeplet--the one who set Joe on a path to locating his mother and convinced him to join the group in order to dismantle the cartel. Jimmy looks up and nods.

"Tell Widow it will be followed to the letter."

The man speaks softly. "Your father, Dave, would have been proud of you. When did you learn it was your father who was our inside man and responsible for the death of Joe's father and his team?"

Jimmy ignores the question and stares coldly into the man's eyes. "Our family will continue to do anything to support the cause."

The man reaches forward and shakes Jimmy's hand. "Widow will be happy to hear this. Goodbye for now."

TWENTY

Joe and Christina have nearly stabilized and are floating together in space. He supports her while she gets her space legs.

"Use your lateral control and adjust 5 degrees. Adjust your horizontal pitch 2 degrees."

She does so and steadies herself. "Okay, Joe, how do you know so much about all this stuff? I never heard of any training in the company that covered this. Hell, I'm not even sure who you are anymore."

"I promise I will tell you everything. But for now, I am sorry I didn't trust you."

"Is that why you started to act weird? What made you stop trusting me?"

"The letter from my... mother. It warned me not to trust you. I... after all these years with no family... I just, um..." Joe becomes quiet. She sees him reflecting.

"Joe, I'm sorry about your folks. We didn't know. We were set up as much as you were."

"You know what, Christina?"

"What?"

"My parents may be gone, but I still have a chance to finish what they started. And I'm going to make sure those bastards pay for their deaths. You with me?"

"Until death does us apart."

"Wow! Small steps... Real small steps... Okay... Baby steps... Did I say small steps?"

Christina laughs as Joe continues. "Let's kill some bad guys first, okay?"

Christina is about to say something when Joe fires his boosters. Christina looks at him leaving. "I love you, Joe," she says softly, feeling relieved to have said the words even if Joe didn't hear them.

The tension and temperature inside the station mount by the second. A handful of dedicated guards continue to stand watch over the ship and the remaining unblocked exits.

Joe and Christina float undetected in the open door of the docking bay. The gentle ripple of the force field is silent and no alarms sound. They quietly land behind the ship. As they take off their suits, Joe points to a guard. She nods, knowing exactly what she is to do. He points to the other one and then to himself. He holds up his fist. Then he counts off one... two... three...

They emerge as one from behind the ship and without hesitation open fire, killing the guards. A quick scan of the area reveals there are no more guards. They climb into the spaceship, closing the hatch behind them.

Joe looks at his watch as he throws switches. "Shit. We have 30 seconds. I need your help."

There is no answer. Joe looks over and sees Christina staring forward without blinking. Joe checks to see what she is looking at. She is staring into deep space. Christina, looking airsick and weakly, says, "Not again."

Joe smiles and starts to call out a sequence to fire the rockets. The engines ignite and the ship blasts out of the dock, leaving a vapor trail in its wake. The satellites are at full power and the beams are intensifying. The station is glowing red-hot, and soon the glow turns from red to white. The station is engulfed in a bright glow as it pulsates to the sounds of metal being stressed to the max. The screeching sounds of malfunctioning equipment intensify and mix together with the terrified screams of people being cooked alive. The station has reached its structural limits. It continues to expand like a balloon, teetering on the verge of the inevitable pop.

Inevitably it can take no more and the station explodes, the heat waves expanding rapidly in concentric circles away from the epicenter. Out of the center of the fireball another ship slingshots itself safely away from the destruction and the rocketing debris. It spins out of control for a short while then settles into a stable attitude.

Inside the craft is Widow, drenched in perspiration. She begins to relax at having escaped and smiles at the thought she will be able to continue her mission. With the ship stabilized, her attention turns to her prized possession. Scanning her surroundings, her eyes stop on the console. Sitting there in full view against a star-filled background is a hermetically sealed canister labeled "DNA-ADOLPH HITLER."

Smiling, she speaks to the vial adoringly. "Soon, my love, soon you will be back with us." She flies off in the opposite direction of Joe and Christina.

The buzz in the NASA control room has escalated. A large tracking monitor showing the moon has unidentifiable debris heading into space. The shapes resemble rockets launching from the lunar surface. The watch commander is very nervous.

"Is that a launch?"

"I'm not sure, sir. We have extreme thermal activity."

"What kind of extreme thermal activity?"

Lana jumps on the computer and starts punching keys. "Sir, we have confirmation that there has been a large explosion."

More information comes across her computer screen, and she hesitates before speaking again... "Sir, it is coming from behind the moon."

"Any idea as to the cause?"

As she continues to type, she says, "Yes, sir. It is our laser satellites that targeted something."

General Bedard turns to the watch commander with anticipated curiosity. "A new development?"

Trying to ignore the general's comments, he says, "And... results, Andrews?"

"Whatever it was, it has been destroyed. According to this data, temperatures reached in access of 7,000 degrees."

Relieved, he says, "Have our defenses stand down."

"Yes, sir."

He is visibly shaken by the experience. "Jesus. What the hell was up there?"

General Bedard shoots the watch commander a shocked expression. "You mean to tell me you don't know?"

Lana looks at the both of them. "Let's hope it wasn't ours."

The idea hits the watch commander and General Bedard hard.

"I think I need a drink. Join me, general?"

"Make mine a double."

The stars mix with glowing objects from the explosion, creating a sensational display of color. The heat ring looks like a circular rainbow filled with more colors than the human brain can perceive. The entire space is filled with shooting stars of debris passing through vapor pockets that ignite temporarily from the extreme temperatures.

Its beauty overwhelms Christina as she stares out the small window of the escape ship. "My God, it is beautiful."

"It makes you want to believe, doesn't it? I guess we should change course and head towards Earth."

"Let's just float for a while. Look at it as our first vacation together."

Joe looks at her and smiles. "Why not? After all, there is nothing left for us to..."

He is cut off mid-sentence as he is smashed in the face and knocked out. Christina turns to see Deswick standing there pointing a weapon at her.

"Nice to see you again. Planning on going somewhere without me?"

Christina checks Joe's pulse.

"It was only a love tap. Besides, I want to kill him after he sees you die."

"Do you practice at being an asshole or does it come naturally?"

Deswick punches Christina in the face, leaving a bloody lip. "Now that I have your attention, un-strap yourself and come with me."

She does. "Where are you taking me?"

"Let's just say the garbage that is jettisoned will have another piece of trash to go along for the ride."

Christina takes a swing at him. He stops her fist inches from his face. Deswick is out of patience. He shoves her hard toward the lower deck, leaving Joe out cold in the cockpit.

Christina and Deswick make their way through the ship and eventually stand in front of a door. He pushes several buttons and the door opens. Inside is all manner of refuse and other objects for disposal.

Deswick smiles. "Along with this garbage you will be compressed into a neat little parcel. This will not kill you, only make you wish you were dead."

"Is this fun for you?"

"No. The real fun starts after this stuff is compressed. A plastic container encloses it all. Next, that door is opened and the parcel is released into space. The oxygen in the container is good for about two minutes. Then you will slowly suffocate."

Christina stares at him in disbelief. "You are a charmer, aren't you? You must get a lot of dates."

Deswick pushes her into the room. Lights begin to flash as a computer voice makes an announcement.

"Auto-destruct sequence has been activated. You have three minutes till self-destruct. Use the emergency escape pod."

Deswick turns toward the front of the ship, realizing what Joe has initiated. "That bastard." He turns to Christina. "Sorry, I will not be able to watch you from here. However, I will enjoy seeing you die from the cockpit with your boyfriend."

The door closes. Christina brings her face up to the window and gives him the finger. The room begins to close in. Christina looks for a way out, but it is hopeless.

Deswick runs into the cockpit with his gun drawn. Joe is gone. He goes over to the control panel and types a series of commands.

The computer comes online. "Please identify yourself and provide your authorization code to cancel auto-destruct."

"Deswick. Adolf 1 9 3 8."

"Auto-destruct canceled."

The container is on the verge of crushing Christina. She can barely turn in a circle. She knows it is only a matter of seconds before she cannot move at all, then the pod will be jettisoned into space, where she will meet with an agonizing death. Her thoughts go to Joe and how close they were to having a chance at a real life together. She closes her eyes and says a final prayer. She takes a long, deep breath. Suddenly her body is jerked roughly as a hand reaches in and pulls her out.

She looks up. "Joe..." She hugs him.

Joe's face contorts. "OOH, you smell... great." They laugh.

"What about Deswick?"

"I knew he would stop the auto-destruct sequence. We have to get off this ship."

She looks at him. "Not again."

"What?"

"You really know how to show a girl a good time."

"Hey, who else could offer you the stars?"

She takes a deep breath. "Okay... Where to now, cowboy?"

"We'll have to use the emergency pod. We will land somewhere near..." He smiles at her. "Fiji."

She brightens at the thought. "Now that's a vacation."

Deswick slowly moves down a hallway with his weapon drawn. He is ready to shoot anything that moves. He arrives at the pod room and as he sees Joe and Christina closing the pod door he realizes that he is too late. "NOOOOOO!" He begins to push buttons when the computer voice comes on again.

"Pod room is now decompressed. The door is sealed. Launch in 5 4 3 2 1."

The ship gently rocks as the pod separates from the ship. From his vantage point Deswick sees Joe and Christina waving goodbye.

Inside the ship Joe's voice comes over a speaker.

"Hey, Deswick, I left a surprise for you in the control room."

Deswick runs down the hallway into the control room. He looks around but doesn't see anything. Christina and Joe watch the ship getting smaller the farther away they get.

"Joe, what was that about a surprise?"

"One good turn deserves another."

"Meaning?"

Joe talks into the microphone. "Hey, Des, ask your computer how life support is doing?"

Deswick stands up and turns toward the escaping pod. Calmly he says, "Computer, life support analysis."

"There are 15 seconds of compressed oxygen left."

Deswick's eyes fill with hatred and terror.

Christina takes the microphone from Joe. "Goodbye, asshole."

The computer voice counts, "7... 6... 5... 4... 3... 2... 1... 0..."

Joe and Christina watch as the ship compresses like an aluminum can as the air is sucked out.

Deswick gives one last salute. "Heil Hitler."

The ship completely collapses inward and the remaining lights go out. Deswick's dying screams echo forever through the vacuum of outer space, and the lifeless craft goes dark, blending with blackness of the void.

Surgeon and the rest of the team are studying data and holograms of the station explosion. Rachel is the first to notice something.

"Sir, we have analyzed this data and enhanced all views, and there seems to be an inconsistency."

Surgeon goes over to the hologram. "What exactly am I looking at?"

"You see this object here?"

"Yes. It appears to be a piece of the station debris."

"Normally I would agree, but there is just one problem."

"And that is?"

"I am going to run this again and slow it down 100 times. Please observe." Rachel starts the hologram, which moves almost frame by frame. The station goes from red hot to white hot.

"As you can clearly see, the station has now reached critical mass and is about to explode."

She advances it again. "Here is the moment of annihilation. But if you enhance the image you see what in regular motion would appear to be part of the station coming apart, except at this point the station has not yet begun to break up."

"Therefore, you conclude something was launched?"

"Not exactly, sir. I took that specific piece of footage and enhanced it as far as it would go."

She adjusts some of the controls and the image in question becomes enlarged. Then slowly the image becomes sharper. Surgeon's eyebrows go up.

"A spaceship?"

"Exactly."

"And you are sure this is not the one carrying Joe and Christina?"

"Correct, sir. In this perspective..." She changes views. "We see the signature of the ship we originally tracked to the moon, which had Joe and Christina aboard. This other ship is carrying someone in the cartel."

"Excellent work, Rachel. Do we have a projected telemetry of the ship?"

"Yes, sir. However, since we discovered this a little late, our field operatives would only be able to retrieve the ship, and the probability of a target being found is very low."

Surgeon thinks for a moment. "Agreed. Have the ship sterilized and report where it touched down. At least we will have the point of departure, which may give us some clues."

"Sir, one more thing."

"Yes, Rachel."

"We tracked the other ship, and our field operatives did not find Joe and Christina onboard."

"What about their codes? Has anyone tried to contact them through the network?"

"Yes, sir, and there was no luck."

"Any sign of foul play at the contact point?"

"No, sir. The area is clean."

"Any ideas?"

"The only conclusion we have come up with is that they must have either experienced a malfunction and did an emergency escape, or the ship was launched by the cartel to expose a field operative and Joe and Christina died in the explosion."

Surgeon doesn't know what to say. "Keep looking into all possibilities. I want something concrete. They are good agents, and I want some answers."

"Yes, sir."

It is a picture-perfect summer night sky, the full moon occasionally eclipsed by a few wispy clouds. A gentle breeze is blowing, and the sounds of night creatures fill the air. A shooting star crosses the sky. Christina points at it.

"Look, Joe."

"It really is beautiful."

Christina sighs. "I could stay here for the rest of our lives."

Joe clears his throat. "You know, Surgeon and operations will be looking for us."

"I know, but you did promise me this vacation, so let's enjoy it for a while, okay?"

Joe and Christina sit in lounge chairs surrounded by lit tiki torches. Behind them is a beautiful resort. Colorfully dressed musicians play for them. This is Wakaya, Fiji. A few couples walk barefoot along the beach under the light of the full moon. Christina snuggles closer to Joe. They sit quietly for a while, taking in the peace and quiet.

Joe opens the locket and looks at the picture of his parents. He gently touches it, wishing things had turned out differently. He closes the locket when he feels Christina rubbing his arm. They share a few minutes of tender silence before Christina decides to ask something that has been constantly on her mind.

"Joe, you know who I am. And you know how I feel about you. Now I need to know about you. Remember, you promised to explain, so let's start easy. Who are you?"

Joe takes a deep breath. He thinks about all they have been through and where he hopes they are headed. His mind still reels with unanswered questions about his past and now about his future. He turns to her with a smile.

"The name's Bond, James Bond."

Christina rolls her eyes and smiles, knowing it will be a while before she gets it out of him. She is about to ask him something else when a waiter walks up.

"Excuse me, would you like another cocktail before your table is ready?

"Yes, please."

As the waiter leaves Christina jumps up from the lounge chair and looks at Joe, her hair flowing in front of her face. One look at her and countless possibilities flash through his mind.

Her full lips separate slowly and purposefully. "You know what I want to do?"

"I have no idea with you."

She stands up and begins taking off her clothes. Joe swallows hard, looks around to see if anyone is watching, and is about to sit up to join her when she turns away from him and heads toward the sea, continuing to drop articles of clothing along the way.

"Go for a swim."

Joe sits there for a moment debating with himself. Then he jumps up and begins to undress. He stops, places the locket and cross on his chair, and then runs after her.

"Wait for me. Hey, is that a shark I see?"

Christina screams, "Stop that. And come here."

When Joe reaches her, they laugh, splash each other, and then finally embrace in a long overdue and hard-won kiss.

Surrendering to the blissful moment, Joe remains totally unaware that on his chair, inside the locket, are the keys to his past, his future, and the sum total of the information his mother and father died protecting. Inside the locket are the Secrets.

ABOUT THE AUTHOR

John Callas is a veteran writer/director/producer in the entertainment business. His experience ranges from the worldwide release of feature films to numerous motion picture trailers, national and international commercials, live action title sequences, laser disc projects, a documentary shot on location in Russia, as well as having been the Worldwide VP for The Walt Disney Company while working at a large post production facility. John recently wrote and directed the feature film "No Solicitors" starring Eric Roberts and is currently adapting NY Times bestselling author, William H LaBarge's book, "Lightning Strikes Twice."

John's prowess can be seen on live action teasers for Ransom, Dennis The Menace, Body Of Evidence, The

Golden Child, Spaceballs, The Glass Menagerie, Cocoon II, Poltergeist III, Betrayed, My Girl, Glenngarry Glenn Ross, As Well As Title Sequences For The Two Jakes and A Few Good Men and a promotional film for an amusement ride from Showscan. John also directed an award-winning short film THE WHITE GORILLA.

While creating live action teasers for feature films, John had the opportunity to work with notable actors including Mel Gibson, Walter Matthau, Jack Nicholson, Madonna, Eddie Murphy and Mel Brooks. In addition to working on feature film teasers, his work can be seen in projects for HBO, The Disney Channel, Show Time, the Broadway Play Phantom Of The Opera and the 1993 redesigned TRISTAR LOGO.

John's extensive background also includes over 200 commercials for such clients as Kellogg's, Dodge, Sunkist, Sprite, Toyota, Fuji, Volkswagen, Honda, McDonalds, Mazda, Minolta, Jedi Merchandising, Kraft, Jordache, Sea World, Givenchy and Sonassage with celebrity George Burns and industrial projects for Corporations including Vidal Sassoon, Salomon North America, Nissan and The Kao Corporation Of Japan.

John's television experience includes directing a 14-week series entitled Potentials, with guests Buckminster Fuller, Norman Cousins, Ray Bradbury, Gene Roddenberry, Timothy Leary and others. He also directed 80 segments for Bobby's World, which has been rated the #1 show on Fox 11 Television in its time slot; garnering John an Emmy nomination.

A multi-faceted filmmaker, John's work can be seen in music videos for Glenn Frey Of The Eagles, Bill Wyman Of The Rolling Stones, Jefferson Starship,

Sammy Hagar, Rick Springfield, Doobie Brothers, Styx and more.

For his work John has been recognized with: An EMMY nomination for *Bobby's World*, THE NEW YORK CRITICS CHOICE AWARD for *Lone Wolf*, several awards for his short *THE WHITE GORILLA*, A CLIO and BELDING for his work on the *Sunkist* campaign, the prestigious BEST OF THE WEST for his directorial work on a one-woman show, and an MTV AWARD FOR BEST CONCEPT for Glen Frey's *Smuggler's Blues*.

John holds a Master Degree from Occidental College, and is a member of The Directors Guild Of America.

www.ingramcontent.com/pod-product-compliance
Lightning Source LLC
Chambersburg PA
CBHW070823120626
46556CB00002B/632